HEROIN
RISKS

Peggy J. Parks

ReferencePoint
Press®

San Diego, CA

© 2021 ReferencePoint Press, Inc.
Printed in the United States

For more information, contact:
ReferencePoint Press, Inc.
PO Box 27779
San Diego, CA 92198
www.ReferencePointPress.com

LIBRARY OF CONGRESS CATALOGING-IN-PUBLICATION DATA

Names: Parks, Peggy J., 1951- author.
Title: Heroin risks / by Peggy J. Parks.
Description: San Diego, CA : ReferencePoint Press, Inc., [2020] | Series:
   Drug risks | Includes bibliographical references and index.
Identifiers: LCCN 2020011935 (print) | LCCN 2020011936 (ebook) | ISBN
   9781682829059 (library binding) | ISBN 9781682829066 (ebook)
Subjects: LCSH: Heroin--United States--Juvenile literature. | Drug
   addiction--United States--Juvenile literature.
Classification: LCC HV5822.H4 P37 2020 (print) | LCC HV5822.H4 (ebook) |
   DDC 362.29/3--dc23
LC record available at https://lccn.loc.gov/2020011935
LC ebook record available at https://lccn.loc.gov/2020011936

CONTENTS

An Illicit, Deadly Drug

What Is Heroin?

Heroin is one of a class of drugs known as opioids. It is made by chemically altering morphine, a natural substance that comes from opium poppy plants that are grown in remote, mountainous areas of the world. Heroin can be a powder or a dark, sticky substance known as black tar heroin. Common street names for heroin are H, Big H, horse, chiva, brown sugar, China white, junk, skunk, smack, hell dust, and white horse. People use heroin primarily by injecting it into a vein, or they may smoke or snort it.

There was a time not so long ago when heroin was rarely talked about. It was considered a frightening, even secretive, drug, which was used mainly by derelicts who were shooting up in abandoned buildings, on dark street corners, and in alleyways. These were considered the typical heroin junkies—the only people desperate enough to stick a needle in an arm and shoot up to get high. But while such stereotypes may (or may not) have been accurate in the past, they are certainly not reality anymore. "The image of a . . . heroin addict collapsed in a filthy dark alley is obsolete," says the Foundation for a Drug-Free World. "Today, the young addict could be 12 years old, play video games and enjoy the music of his generation."[1]

Although the number of twelve-year-old heroin addicts is low, the foundation's point is that old-fashioned stereotypes about heroin users have been shattered. Males and females of all ages, ethnicities, and walks of life are using heroin—often to the detriment of their health, their relationships, and their lives.

An Alarming Situation

Heroin is part of a family of drugs known as opioids. These drugs are also called narcotics, which is a term derived from Greek words for "numb" and "stupor." The opioid family includes prescription painkillers, such as Vicodin, OxyContin, and Percocet; counterfeit versions of these drugs, which are sold illicitly on the street; and heroin.

Opioids block pain signals between the brain and the body, producing an unnatural high that makes users feel relaxed and happy. "Heroin is seductive," says former heroin addict Ben Cimon. "The minute it hits you, all your worries disappear. You are content with everything. You feel warm. You can't help but smile. You feel free. The first time I tried it, I found an escape from the feelings of sadness and isolation I had been experiencing for as long as I could remember." When Cimon became addicted to heroin, he learned that feeling "free" was a delusion. "Once heroin gets a hold on you, it never lets go,"[2] he comments.

—Ben Cimon, a young man who was addicted to heroin

Heroin has always been a dangerous drug, but in recent years it has become deadlier than ever. That is because illicit drug producers are cutting it with a powerful synthetic opioid known as fentanyl, which is at least fifty times more potent than heroin. According to the National Institute on Drug Abuse (NIDA), fentanyl is cheap to produce, which is why it is often mixed in with heroin—dealers make more money that way. And while they continue to get richer, people are dying

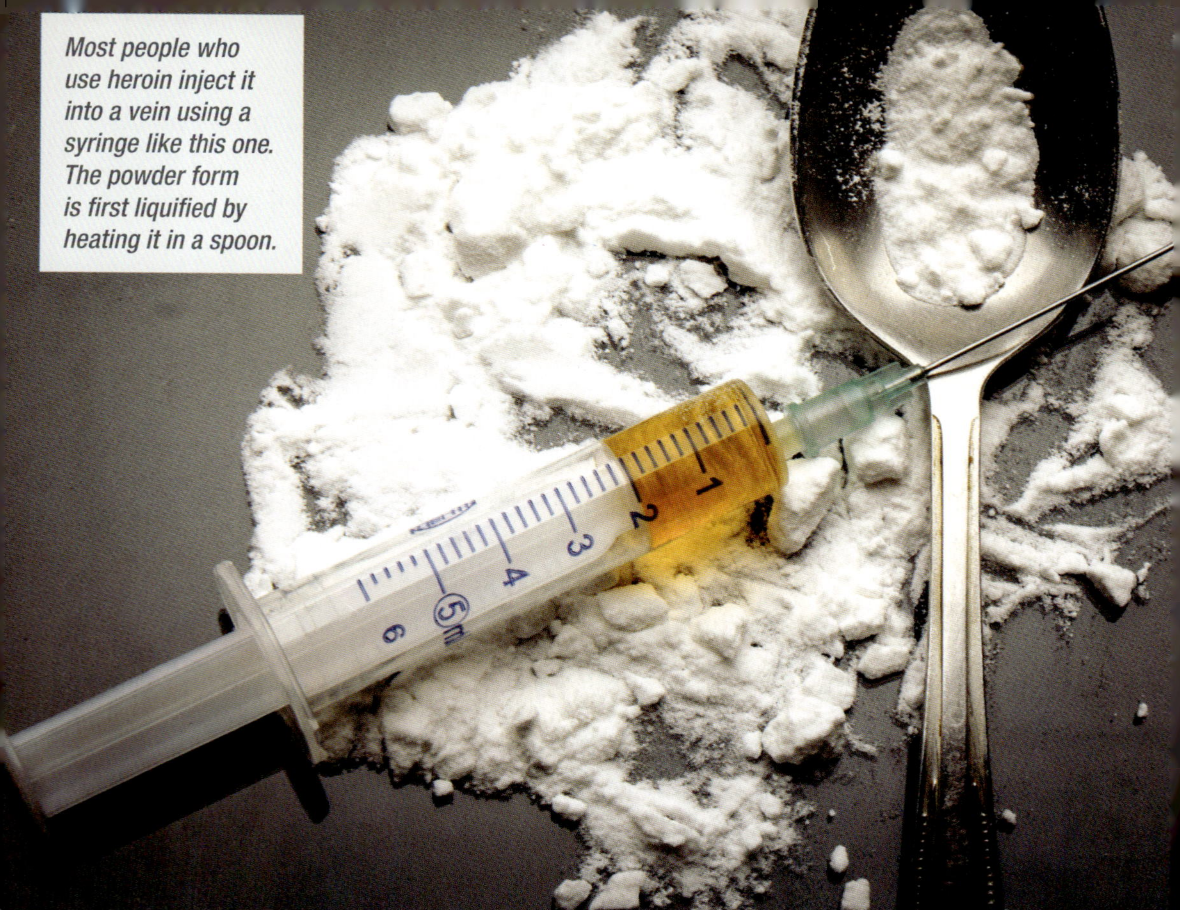

from overdoses at unprecedented rates. They use heroin and are often unaware that it has been cut with a drug so powerful and deadly that only a few grains can kill them. "With any given drug purchase, people don't know what they're getting," says physician and public health researcher Daniel Ciccarone. "It's sadly like 'Russian roulette.'"[3]

When Heroin Was Medicine

Today there is no question that heroin is dangerous and addictive—as well as illegal to purchase, possess, and use—under all circumstances. But this was not always the case. In the 1890s the pharmaceutical company Bayer introduced heroin as a nonaddictive substitute for morphine. It was also added to aspirin and sold in glass bottles clearly labeled with the word *heroin*. Shockingly, the heroin/aspirin was also marketed as a treatment for sick children who suffered from fever, coughs, and sore throats from colds. Some of the ads, targeted at mothers, showed children eagerly reaching for the bottles that contained the heroin/aspirin.

By the early 1900s heroin addiction statistics made it clear that scientists were terribly wrong in believing that heroin was nonaddictive. Government officials took action, and by 1924 the drug was banned under US law. Still, the damage was done. The widespread acceptance of heroin's use had led to a huge increase in addiction. Over the years, the addiction rates fluctuated and decreased substantially, only to rise again during the 2000s because of the proliferation of opioids.

The Crisis Continues

As the opioid crisis rages on in the United States, health officials and addiction experts are distressed as well as perplexed about how to stop it—and there are no simple answers. Heroin claims a tragic number of lives each year, with no end in sight. According to the Centers for Disease Control and Prevention (CDC), overdose deaths involving heroin rose from 1,960 in 1999 to 15,482 in 2017—a nearly 700 percent increase. The drug that was once sold as a remedy for feverish children is now a deadly contributor to the worst drug crisis in US history.

CHAPTER ONE

A Nationwide Problem

The opioid problem in the United States has become a full-blown crisis in recent years, and heroin plays a major part in that. Often, the drug's use is rooted in the abuse of prescription opioid painkillers. Many people who became addicted to these pills and were no longer able to get them legitimately were desperate to find a replacement—and they found it in heroin. Not only was it much cheaper to buy on the street, but it was also easier to get from dealers. Those who had long considered heroin to be a taboo drug, one they would never dream of using, found themselves addicted to it. Thus, there has been a huge and alarming spike in heroin addiction and overdose deaths in the United States since 2010. "Our nation's heroin and opioid crisis has become more and more horrific,"[4] says opioid expert Daniel Ciccarone.

A Dangerous, Addictive Drug

As deadly as heroin is, some people might be surprised to learn that it is derived from a beautiful flowering plant. Indeed, massive fields of bright-red *Papaver somniferum* (opium poppies) are grown in remote, mountainous regions of the world, primarily in southern Asia and parts of Latin America, where climates are warm and dry. When the plants mature, the blossoms drop off, exposing large egg-shaped seed pods. These pods are harvested and sliced open for their milky sap, which contains raw opium. The opium can be refined to make morphine, which has legitimate medical use as a potent painkilling drug. Or, if the intent is illicit, morphine may be chemically processed and made into heroin. Although morphine and heroin are officially known as opiates, the word *opioids*, originally designating synthetic opiates, has become an umbrella term that is often used to refer to both.

Heroin is known by a number of street names, including black tar, chiva, brown sugar, China white, H, Big H, horse, junk, skunk, smack, hell dust, and white horse. What the drug is called often depends on the type. Two main types of heroin have been identified in the United States. Powdered heroin, as the name suggests, is a powder that is usually cut (diluted) with similar-looking substances such as powdered milk, sugar, talcum powder, and cornstarch. Powdered heroin is usually white, but it may be a slightly darker shade depending on what it is cut with and the region it comes from. The other type of heroin is known as black tar heroin. The crude processing methods used to produce this type of heroin leave behind many impurities and create a substance that is sticky, similar to roofing tar.

Where Heroin Comes From

According to the Drug Enforcement Administration (DEA), about 90 percent of the heroin in the United States comes from Mexico. The remainder comes from South America and, to a lesser extent, Southwest Asia. According to the DEA's *2018 National Drug Threat Assessment*, Mexican poppy cultivation increased by 35 percent from 2016 to 2017, and the estimated 108,973 acres (44,100 ha) cultivated in 2017 accounted for about 122 tons (111 metric tons) of pure heroin.

Heroin, along with other illicit drugs like methamphetamine, cocaine, and fentanyl, is smuggled across the US-Mexico border. Contrary to the claims of many politicians, however, most heroin in the United States does not enter the country through open areas along the border. According to Gil Kerlikowske, who served as

The Soaring Rate of Heroin Overdoses

Research has shown that throughout the 1990s the number of deaths related to heroin overdose remained relatively steady. After 2010 the number started trending up, however, and by 2017 it had soared to 15,482 deaths. The following year (2018) the number dropped slightly to 14,996, which health officials hope is a positive sign for the future.

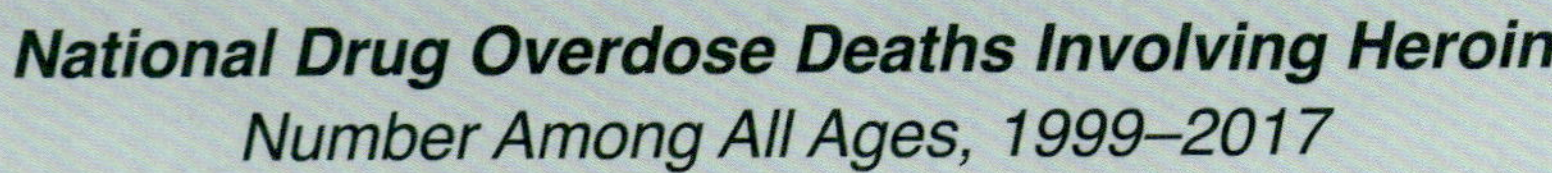

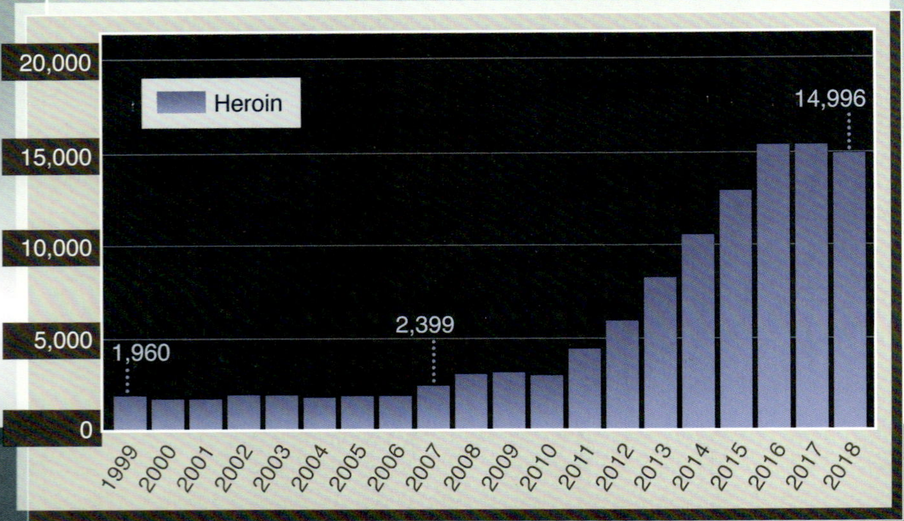

Source: Centers for Disease Control and Prevention, "Data Brief 356: Drug Overdose Deaths in the United States, 1999–2018," January 2020. www.cdc.gov.

director of US Customs and Border Protection (CBP) from 2014 to 2017, more than 90 percent of the illicit narcotics in the United States enters the country through legal ports of entry along the southern border. "People don't backpack or try to sneak those drugs across the border between the ports of entry because . . . they could be caught by the Border Patrol," says Kerlikowske. He explains that it is more common "to have somebody that is taking the drugs through a port of entry where they're met on the other side of the port here in the United States."

Over the past several years, there has been an increase in the amount of heroin being smuggled into the United States. This is largely due to stepped-up production and trafficking of the drug by Mexican cartels, or criminal networks. And, according to the Congressional Research Service, a US public policy research institute, "to facilitate the distribution and sale of drugs in the United States, Mexican drug traffickers have formed relationships with U.S. gangs."[6]

Such efforts have led to an increase not only in trafficking but also in the number of heroin seizures in the country, particularly at the US-Mexico border. The DEA reports that nationwide, 17,590 pounds (7,979 kg) of heroin were seized in 2017. Of that amount, 39 percent, or 6,812 pounds (3,090 kg), was seized at the southwestern border. This represents an increase of almost 55 percent over the approximately 4,409 pounds (2,000 kg) seized a decade prior. The DEA reports that it made more than fifty-four hundred heroin-related arrests in 2017—most of these for trafficking.

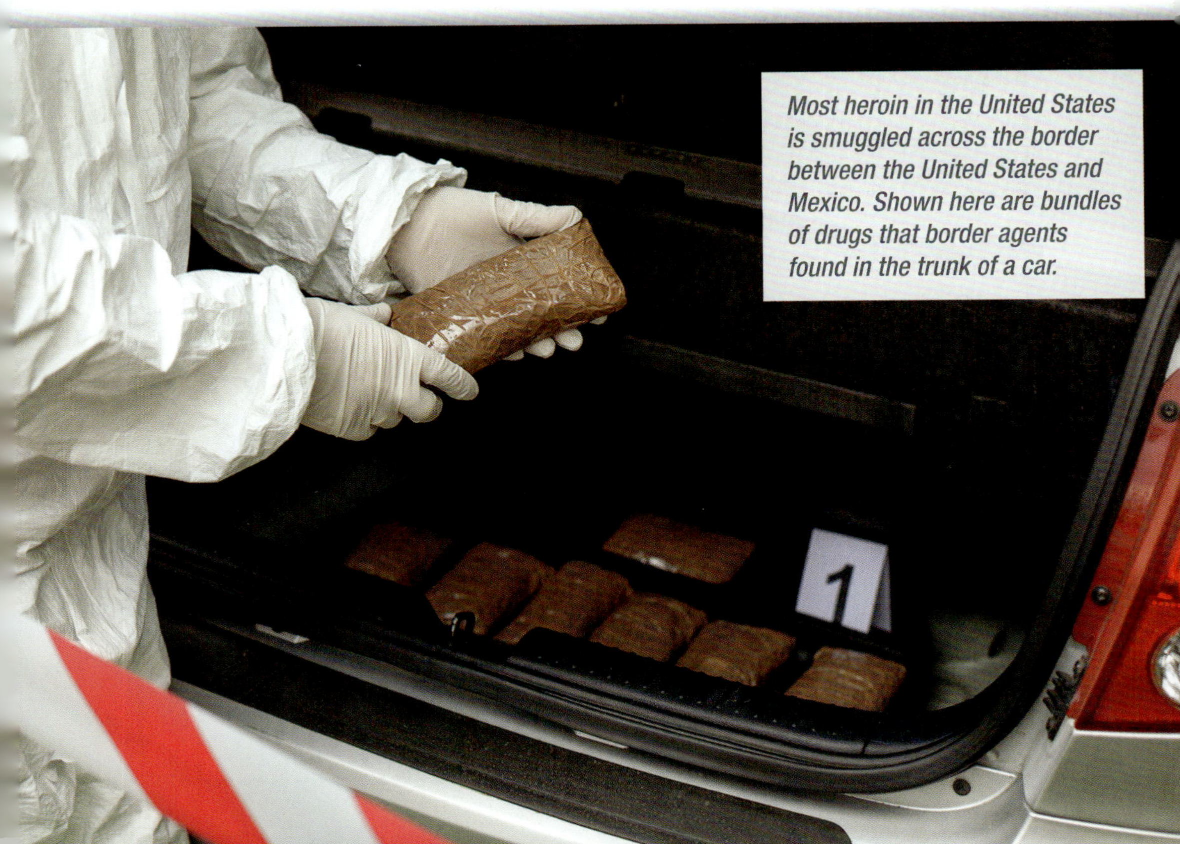

Most heroin in the United States is smuggled across the border between the United States and Mexico. Shown here are bundles of drugs that border agents found in the trunk of a car.

The problem of heroin and other drugs coming across the southern border continues to pose challenges for law enforcement. One of the agencies that works to prevent illicit drugs from crossing the border is CBP. In January 2020, CBP officers on the US side of the bridge connecting Brownsville, Texas, and Matamoros, Mexico, seized a load of cocaine, heroin, and methamphetamine valued at approximately $205,852. Using a nonintrusive imaging system and a canine unit, CBP officers found twenty-six packages containing the illicit narcotics hidden inside a 2011 Chevrolet Cruze. "Our officers did an outstanding job in seizing these hard

Heroin Does Not Discriminate

It is common for people to make assumptions about the *typical* heroin user or the *typical* heroin addict—but their assumptions are often wrong. One person who knows this well is Katie Donovan, whose daughter Brittany started using heroin as a teenager and became addicted to it. "I had skewed images of what a heroin addict looked like," says Donovan. "I envisioned them sitting in an alley, a criminal or stereotypical hippie from the '60s and '70s, someone who grew up in a bad home. I had preconceived notions that you had to stay away from them—that they were *bad* people." She adds, "Never once did I envision my daughter."

After watching Brittany struggle with heroin addiction, Donovan felt ashamed of her long-held judgmental beliefs. Today she writes and speaks about heroin addiction and how it can—and does—affect people of all walks of life. "It's the high school quarterback who became injured in a game," says Donovan, "was prescribed Vicodin, and became addicted. . . . It's the heroic Marine who fought in the Gulf War, who is now fighting PTSD and addiction. . . . It's the senior citizen who had hip surgery, and within weeks, unknowingly grew dependent on prescription narcotics. *It's my daughter.*" Donovan has advice for people who are stuck in judgmental thinking as she was for so long. "Get your head out of the sand," she says. "If you feel like 'it would never happen to you or anyone in your circle,' take a look around. It's happening."

Katie Donovan, "My Daughter the Addict: A Suburban Mom's Nightmare," *Lafayette (LA) Daily Advertiser*, November 28, 2016. www.theadvertiser.com.

narcotics," said Brownsville Port of Entry director Tater Ortiz. "The security of our borders is something that our officers are devoted to and take very seriously."[7]

Methods of Using Heroin

Part of the reason for heroin's growth in popularity is that there are more ways it can be used. In the past, the only way for people to use the drug was to inject it into a vein, which was repugnant to many drug users. Today, although injection is still the primary way heroin is used, it can also be snorted or smoked.

When someone plans to inject heroin, it first must be melted into a liquid, which is then injected into veins or muscles or under the skin with a hypodermic needle, a process known as shooting up. This method provides the fastest high for the user—depending on the injection site, usually within a few seconds to five minutes—because the heroin immediately enters the bloodstream and upon reaching the brain leads to euphoric feelings and numbing sensations throughout the body. Users who repeatedly inject heroin (or any drug) typically develop scars at the injection sites that are known as track marks. These are a telltale sign of chronic intravenous (IV) drug use and often lead to the user being socially stigmatized.

Powdered heroin is usually snorted or smoked, which is typically more appealing to people trying it for the first time. This is because many people are frightened or even repulsed by needles and also because of the stigma associated with shooting up. As the Foundation for a Drug-Free World explains, "A young person who might think twice about putting a needle in his arm may more readily smoke or sniff the same drug."[8] The drug is just as dangerous whether snorted, smoked, or injected.

—Foundation for a Drug-Free World, a nonprofit that seeks to end drug and alcohol abuse

Who Uses Heroin?

According to the CDC, some of the greatest increases in heroin use have occurred in demographic groups "with historically low rates of heroin use: women, the privately insured, and people with higher incomes."[9] According to the 2018 National Survey on Drug Use and Health, an annual survey on the use of legal and illegal drugs in the United States, about 808,000 people aged twelve or older used heroin at some point during the previous year. This number includes about 10,000 adolescents aged twelve to seventeen, 157,000 young adults aged eighteen to twenty-five, and 641,000 adults aged twenty-six and older. These numbers have been on the rise in recent years, with the greatest increases among young adults.

Although heroin use was once solely an urban problem, that is no longer the case. NIDA reports that "the impact of heroin use is felt all across the United States, with heroin being identified as the most or one of the most important drug use issues affecting several local regions from coast to coast."[10] For example, several suburban and rural communities around Chicago, Illinois, and St. Louis, Missouri, have reported an increase in the amount of heroin seized by law enforcement as well as an increase in the number of heroin overdose deaths.

Who Is at Highest Risk for Using Heroin?

Research has shown that the strongest risk factor for becoming a heroin user is prior dependence on prescription opioids, such as Vicodin, OxyContin, and Percocet. Opioid pain medications have effects that are similar to heroin, which NIDA says may be one reason why opioid abuse so often leads to heroin use. An estimated 80 percent of people who use heroin began by abusing prescription opioids. It is important to note, however, that only a small fraction of people who abuse opioid medications go on to use heroin—less than 4 percent, according to data from the National Survey on Drug Use and Health. "This suggests that prescription opioid abuse is just one factor in the pathway to heroin,"[11] explains NIDA.

Indeed, a number of other risk factors for using heroin have been identified. According to the CDC, males, non-Hispanic whites, and eighteen- to twenty-five-year-olds are at higher risk for using heroin, as are people who live in large metropolitan areas. Another strong risk factor is addiction to substances like cocaine, marijuana, and alcohol. Many young people who begin experimenting with alcohol or marijuana have found themselves on a slippery slope toward harder drugs such as heroin. One example is Jesse, a recovered heroin user who began drinking and using marijuana as a youth before moving on to heroin. "When I became old enough to make my own decisions, I often made the wrong ones, and where most may have learned from these mistakes and moved on, I soon became caught in the cycle of addiction," he says. "It started with smoking pot and drinking and soon evolved into harder drugs. Eventually, after some years I ended up struggling to survive as an IV heroin user."[12]

Like Jesse, former heroin addict Nicholette began experimenting with drugs at a young age—only thirteen. Before long she was using heroin, as she explains:

> By the time I had become a freshman in high school I was a regular marijuana smoker, had taken acid on numerous occasions, mushrooms, hash, nitrous [oxide], and had learned how to inhale whatever it is in aerosol cans that gets you high. By the time I was 22, I had added cocaine and heroin to the list, as well as recreationally taking prescription pain medication whenever I had the opportunity since I was 15 years old.[13]

Teenage Heroin Users

The connection between prescription opioids and heroin is especially prominent among adolescents. A 2019 study by researchers at the University of Southern California (USC), published in *JAMA Pediatrics*, focused on this connection. The study, which

Those who start experimenting with alcohol or marijuana as teens have a high risk of turning to harder drugs such as heroin in later years.

was conducted from 2013 to 2017, is the first to track prescription opioid and heroin use over time among a group of teens.

The researchers followed 3,298 freshmen from ten high schools in the Los Angeles area through their senior year. The students were asked about any previous and current abuse of prescription painkillers such as Percocet, OxyContin, and Vicodin to get high. Participants were also asked about any use of heroin or other substances like alcohol, cigarettes, marijuana, and methamphetamine. The researchers found that between 10.7 and 13.1 percent of high school freshmen who were habitual opioid users went on to use heroin by the end of high school. Moreover, the link between prescription opioid abuse and later heroin use was stronger than links between marijuana, alcohol, and methamphetamine and later heroin use. The study also found that only 1.7 percent of teens who did not use prescription opioids to get high later tried heroin by high school graduation.

Of these findings, senior author Adam Leventhal, a professor of preventive medicine and psychology and the director of the USC Institute for Addiction Science at the Keck School of Medicine, comments,

Prescription opioids and heroin activate the brain's pleasure circuit in similar ways. Teens who enjoy the "high" from prescription opioids could be more inclined to seek out other drugs that produce euphoria, including heroin. . . . While we can't definitively conclude that there is a cause-and-effect relation, there may be something unique about opioid drugs that makes youths vulnerable to trying heroin. The results do not appear to be driven by the tendency of some teens to act out, rebel, or experiment with many types of drugs.[14]

The number of teenage heroin addicts in the United States is low compared to other age groups. According to NIDA, past-year heroin use among eighth, tenth, and twelfth graders in the United States is at its lowest levels since 1991, at less than 1 percent in each grade level. Still, when young people do turn to heroin, it is nearly always because they could no longer get prescription pain-killers, and buying them on the street is outrageously expensive. Heroin, in contrast, is a fraction of the cost of prescription opioids.

A Growing Crisis

The issue of heroin use and addiction in the United States is a growing crisis with tragic consequences. The CDC says that between 2010 and 2017, the rate of heroin-related overdose deaths increased by almost 400 percent. Research has shown that there is a strong link between the opioid crisis and the alarming rise in the use of heroin nationwide. In recent years, heroin use has increased among men and women, most age groups, all income levels, and both rural and urban dwellers. With drug trafficking on the rise, stemming the flow of heroin into the nation has become a mammoth task, and the crisis of heroin use has become an epidemic with no easy solutions.

CHAPTER TWO

The Stranglehold of Addiction

Heroin is known to be one of the world's most addictive substances. It is so addictive, in fact, that someone can get hooked on the drug after using it only a few times. No one knows this better than people who have tried heroin thinking that addiction would never happen to them—when the reality is, it can happen to anyone. Heroin's allure is strong and seductive. Once new users find that they like how it makes them feel, or how it helps them escape from their problems, they crave more of it. By giving in to their craving, they unknowingly join the ranks of those who have done the exact same thing and ended up addicted, caught in its stranglehold.

This is a familiar scenario for Deon, a former heroin addict. He grew up in a chaotic household with a neglectful, alcoholic mother and her abusive boyfriend. Deon was only ten years old when he started stealing from his mother's stash of alcohol and drinking to escape from his horrible home environment. He continued to drink and use drugs throughout his teenage years. By the time he was a young adult, he was hooked on heroin—and it proved to be even better at helping him blot out the trauma in his life. "Just after I'd shoot up, I'd get an amazing rush," recalls Deon. "I'd be on top of the world. Once the high really set in, my mind would get slow and fuzzy. It'd feel like I was sinking into the floor. I'd forget if I was asleep or awake, and time just passed me by." Before long, heroin addiction had taken over his life. "After a while, I needed heroin just to get by,"[15] he says.

How Heroin Affects the Brain

The main reason why heroin is so addictive is because of how it affects the brain. Like all opioids, heroin targets the naturally occurring opioid receptors in the brain and other parts of the body. But due to its chemistry, heroin acts much faster than most other drugs. When a person smokes or snorts heroin, and especially when they inject it, the drug enters the bloodstream and travels to the brain in as little as five minutes.

As heroin travels through the bloodstream, it attaches to the opioid receptors. These receptors are located in the brain, in the brain stem, and down the spinal cord, as well as in the lungs and intestines. When the heroin hits receptors, it affects the way the brain processes pain and pleasure. This results in an intense but short rush—a surge of euphoria. The initial rush lasts about five to fifteen minutes and then dwindles to a sense of relaxation and tranquility that can last several hours. "It felt like everything was melting and everything was somehow better," one former heroin user recalls. "Nothing mattered. It lasted about five or six hours and I felt really floaty and nice."[16]

Opioid receptors control more than feelings of pleasure; they also control sensations of pain. Heroin dulls pain in the same way that prescription opioids do: by attaching to opioid receptors and preventing the brain from processing pain signals. Heroin can also temporarily relieve stress, anxiety, and depression. Opioid receptors also control breathing, heart rate, sleeping, and appetite. Heroin slows down a user's breathing and heart rate and leads to drowsiness. It can either suppress or increase a user's appetite, depending on the individual. Other common effects of heroin include clouded thinking, a dry mouth, and a feeling of heaviness in the arms and legs.

Cravings and Tolerance

The high that heroin produces makes the user feel good—until the drug wears off a few hours later. Then depression sets in, and often agitation, and the user desperately wants the good feelings back again. This is how addiction begins. Heroin disrupts the brain's reward system by overwhelming opioid receptors, which leads to immense levels of pleasure. The brain then learns that heroin causes pleasure and happiness, and it produces cravings for the drug. "Any time you start to feel like you're getting antsy or anxious or a little stressed," says one former heroin addict, "your body says it knows exactly how to get out of this, and it's telling you to just go get a little bit more of that heroin."[17]

The opioid receptors in the brain adapt to repeated heroin use by becoming less responsive. This is known as tolerance.

Many people think they can try heroin just to see what it is like and give it up anytime they want; but soon they cannot sleep or relax without it and crave more.

Regular users may feel less pleasure from the drug because their opioid receptors have become less sensitive to heroin's effects. Thus, they need more of the drug, or need it more often, in order to achieve the same levels of pleasure. And as users continue to use more heroin, their opioid receptors continue to adapt, making them even more dependent on the drug. This cycle of increased tolerance leading to increased usage inevitably leads to addiction.

Many people have tried heroin thinking that they will only take it one time just to see what it is like—but before they realize it, they are hooked. "It will cling to you like an obsessed lover," says

Breaking the Cycle

Shane Buffaloe was raised by a single mom and never knew his dad, who was a heroin addict. As a child, this was hard for Buffaloe because he felt abandoned by his dad. "I always wondered how someone could choose drugs over a relationship with their own children," he says. He vowed that when he was older and had a family of his own, he would never do what his father did—yet that proved to be a vow he was unable to keep.

After years of abusing alcohol and drugs, Buffaloe tried heroin when he was in his twenties. He got hooked quickly, and soon his whole life revolved around getting his next fix. "Heroin stole my soul and everything I loved—nothing else mattered," he recalls. His relationship with his three daughters fell apart. He stole money from friends and family members. He stole from stores and spent time in jail. He tried rehab three different times. Finally, Buffaloe was ready to give up. "I didn't want to live with the horrors of drug addiction anymore," he says "The pain was so great . . . I just wanted to die." Buffaloe made up his mind to intentionally overdose—and then he thought about his daughters, and what his suicide would do to them. "I had an unexplainable moment of clarity," he remembers. He got help, beat his addiction, and now shares his story with others who are struggling just as he had.

Shane Buffaloe, "I Was the Father with a Needle in His Arm: How I Took My Life Back from Heroin," *Chicago Tribune*, March 22, 2018. www.chicagotribune.com.

Sam, a fifteen-year-old addict. "The rush of the hit and the way you'll want more, as if you were being deprived of air—that's how it will trap you."[18]

The Addicted Brain

People who develop a tolerance to heroin need more and more of it, which signals the brain to create additional opioid receptors to process the ever-increasing amount of the drug. This change in the brain's structure is why users are unable to replicate the initial euphoric high, and it is also part of the reason why heroin is so addictive. "There is no way for the user's brain to go back to the standard amount of opiate receptors," explains the staff at American Addiction Centers. "It is the process by which the user is compelled to take more and more heroin because there are always more new opiate receptors than there is heroin available."[19]

This was Madeleine Ludwig's experience. She began using heroin shortly after graduating high school and was soon addicted. But the longer she used the drug, the harder it was for her to achieve the blissful high that she craved. "The more often I used it, the more unattainable those initial effects became,"[20] Ludwig says.

Another reason heroin is so highly addictive is that it actually hijacks the brain's reward and pleasure system. In a normally functioning brain, opioid receptors release chemicals known as endorphins (such as dopamine), which act as natural feel-good chemicals and natural painkillers. Heroin interferes with this natural process, throwing the system off and triggering an artificial surge of dopamine into the bloodstream. This process actually rewires circuits in the brain and makes life without heroin very difficult— and even painful. Thus, the user needs more and more of the drug. "The pleasure and reward cycles flip," says *New York Times* reporter Shreeya Sinha. "You get less pleasure from the drug, but want it all the more. The more you seek and take the drug, the more the brain adapts to the drug and demands more."[21]

Heroin activates the release of dopamine much more powerfully than natural rewards such as a happy surprise or a delicious meal do. "Heroin erases the brain's ability to produce its own dopamine and instead takes over how the user perceives pleasure and satisfaction,"[22] explains the staff at American Addiction Centers. Heroin fools the brain into thinking that the drug is necessary for survival. It also lowers users' self-control and decision-making ability—leading those who are desperate for the drug to do almost anything to get more.

Brain Research

Because of how dangerous and addictive heroin and other opioids are, scientists are researching how they affect the brain's structure. One 2019 study, for instance, focused on how the brain is affected by regular exposure to heroin—and what the study revealed was profound.

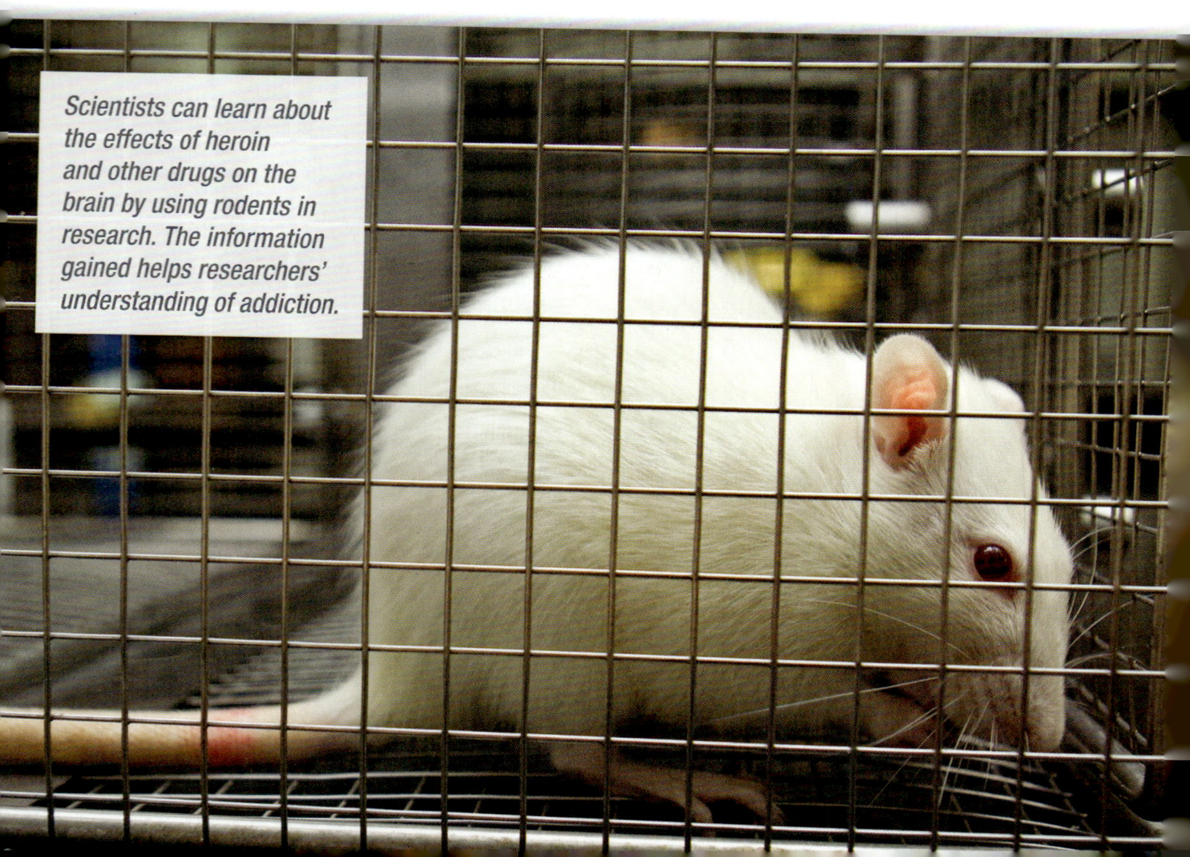

Scientists can learn about the effects of heroin and other drugs on the brain by using rodents in research. The information gained helps researchers' understanding of addiction.

Researchers at the State University of New York at Buffalo conducted the study with rodents. Studying the creatures' brains enabled them to examine synapses, which are tiny spaces between nerve cells that allow the cells to "communicate" by passing rapid-fire electrical signals to one another. The researchers focused on the mechanisms behind addiction and relapse. Specifically, they studied how changes in the synapses can affect a heroin user's potential for relapse after going off the drug.

They found that heroin use drastically reduces levels of drebrin, which is the protein needed to develop and maintain the synapses. Reductions of drebrin affect the cells that are involved in the brain's reward and pleasure pathways. Prior research has shown that loss of the protein is associated with brain diseases such as Alzheimer's disease and Down syndrome. Because of that association, as well as drebrin's known involvement in developing and maintaining brain synapses, the researchers "wondered if it was also involved in addiction to drugs of abuse,"[23] explains neuroscientist and lead study author David Dietz.

Another key finding was that opiate exposure rewires synapses in the brain and decreases the parts of neurons that play a key role in neuronal transmission, learning, and memory. In essence, says Dietz, "opiates fundamentally change how the brain communicates with itself."[24]

—David Dietz, a neuroscientist with the State University of New York at Buffalo

The Excruciating Pain of Withdrawal

For those addicted to heroin, going without a fix can lead to devastating physical withdrawal from the drug. In fact, withdrawal can be so agonizing that people who are addicted to heroin seek out the drug mainly to avoid the terrible physical consequences of not using it. Ludwig remembers this well, as she explains: "Once I had an everyday habit, I was no longer using for the calming effects. I was using to avoid a painful physical withdrawal."[25]

NIDA says that heroin withdrawal may occur within a few hours after the drug has been taken—usually within twelve hours of the last dose—and peak within twenty-four to forty-eight hours. People with less severe addictions may experience withdrawal for only a few days, whereas those with strong, longer-term addictions may suffer for up to a week if they remain off the drug.

The symptoms of heroin withdrawal may include restlessness, muscle and bone pain, insomnia, diarrhea, vomiting, severe chills and cold flashes with goose bumps on the skin, jerky leg movements, and severe cravings for the drug. Ludwig shares her own personal heroin withdrawal horror story:

> The physical withdrawal was fiercely uncomfortable. It would start a nervous tick, such as excessive yawning or sneezing. Symptoms would progress to body aches and stomach pain. After several hours of not using, the constipating effects of heroin would wear off, causing uncontrollable diarrhea. Hot and cold sweats, restless legs, vomiting, lack of appetite and severe body pains caused insomnia that made the withdrawal even more miserable.[26]

Heroin addicts describe withdrawal as so terrible, so excruciatingly painful, that dying would be preferable. Deon went through such a dreadful time while withdrawing from heroin that he has trouble putting his thoughts into words. "Too long without a fix, and . . . I can't even describe it," he says. "It's like I was dying in every awful way you could think of, all at once. Pain in all my bones, throwing up, chills, and I couldn't sleep for days."[27]

As horrific as the physical symptoms of heroin withdrawal can be, the psychological effects can be equally unbearable. These may include depression, anxiety, and feelings of total despair. "I think one of the most difficult parts is

The Myth of the "Addictive Personality"

Research has shown that some people are more vulnerable to addiction than others. Childhood trauma, genetics, peer pressure, and family environment are all factors that have been associated with addiction to heroin or other drugs. Another factor that some believe increases vulnerability to drug addiction is having an "addictive personality," which is often described as an individual's natural tendency to become addicted, whether to alcohol, cigarettes, drugs, technology, or shopping. The theory further holds that because of addictive personality, someone who has recovered from addiction will always be at risk of becoming addicted again.

According to physician Peter Grinspoon, however, the addictive personality theory is a myth and has no basis in scientific evidence. Grinspoon himself recovered from opioid addiction in 2007. While in rehab, he was lectured repeatedly about how someone with an addictive personality has a high risk of getting addicted to most anything:

> I was told on a daily basis that "a drug is a drug is a drug.". . . Personally, I am skeptical that many people substitute addictions. In my experience, people who are addicted tend to have a particular affinity for a particular class of drug, not for *all* drugs and alcohol. This is probably based on some combination of their neurochemistry and their psychological makeup. I was addicted to opiates, but didn't have difficulties with substances in other classes. I have seen this to mostly be the case with thousands of my brothers and sisters in recovery who I have had the honor to interact with.

Peter Grinspoon, "Does Addiction Last a Lifetime?," *Harvard Health Blog,* October 8, 2018. www.health.harvard.edu.

the mental withdrawal," says Marc Myer, the director of the Health Care Professionals Program at Hazelden Betty Ford Foundation in Center City, Minnesota. Myer describes mental withdrawal as a combination of "a severe depression and feeling that you're never going to pull out of that state."[28]

The staff at American Addiction Centers describes the psychological aspects of heroin withdrawal as "mentally crippling, forcing a user into thinking that being off heroin is a desolate state of existence, and the only way to feel good again is by getting high and finding the warmth and peacefulness of a hit."[29]

Born Addicted

One of the most devastating aspects of the heroin epidemic is how it harms the most vulnerable victims: babies whose mothers use heroin during pregnancy. The effects can include premature birth, low birth weight, birth defects, and stillbirth (dead at birth). Heroin use during pregnancy can also lead to a serious condition known as placental abruption, in which the placenta, which supplies the baby with food and oxygen, separates from the wall of the uterus before birth. Placental abruption can result in heavy bleeding and can be deadly for both the baby and the mother.

Babies who are born to mothers who used heroin during pregnancy can be born addicted to the drug—and suffer from the same horrific withdrawal that adult heroin addicts describe. According to NIDA, every fifteen minutes a baby is born suffering from withdrawal from heroin or other opioids. The babies are tormented; they tremble and writhe, cry constantly, and are inconsolable because their tiny bodies crave drugs. "He's frantic," says Dr. Stefan Maxwell, a neonatologist (a doctor who cares for newborns) in West Virginia, of an infant suffering from withdrawal. "Baby isn't sleeping, isn't eating, isn't growing. It's a disaster. Nurses are in tears at the end of a shift."[30]

Living in Agony

Far too many people have been caught in the grips of the tragedy of heroin addiction. It is a terrible, agonizing affliction that holds its users like a vice. For those who are addicted, getting another fix becomes their sole purpose in life. Most addicts will continue using heroin—even when they no longer enjoy the experience—simply to avoid the dreaded physical and mental effects of withdrawal. Many addicts started out thinking they could try the drug just once, only to find themselves swiftly caught in the stranglehold of addiction.

CHAPTER THREE

Heroin's Destructive Health Effects

Of all the drugs that are known to be harmful, heroin is one of the most devastating. It destroys people's lives, wiping out their ability to care about anything but getting their next fix. And in the process, it destroys their bodies and their sense of well-being. Allie, a woman from Atlanta, Georgia, is living proof of this. Once a teen beauty pageant contestant, Allie now lives for nothing but her $200 per day heroin habit. Allie is in her forties, but she looks twenty years older. Her skin is weathered and wrinkled. She is painfully thin with brittle hair. She is jittery. She has track marks on her arms and the backs of her hands from decades of shooting up. She also has no teeth, which is not unusual for long-term heroin users. "Look at me," she says tearfully during an interview. "I'm not supposed to look like this!"[31] Allie makes it clear that how she looks, and how she feels, is a direct result of being addicted to heroin.

Heroin's Short-Term Effects

Exactly how heroin affects users depends on a number of factors, such as how long someone has been using it and how it is administered. Most users describe feeling a sense of warmth, and sometimes euphoria, followed by sleepiness. But they also may experience unpleasant effects like nausea and vomiting—which can hit suddenly. One former heroin addict recalls shooting up and feeling "different waves of warmth" throughout his body, and then "all of a sudden I hurled into the [garbage] bin."[32]

Other unpleasant effects of heroin include dry mouth, very itchy skin, and a heavy feeling in the arms and legs. Users often experience clouded mental functioning, difficulty concentrating, and slurred speech. It is also common, after someone has used, to alternate between states of drowsiness and wakefulness, which is called being "on the nod." Opioid expert Daniel Ciccarone likens this to someone who is extremely sleepy and trying hard to stay awake. The person's head nods and drops down as he gets sleepier, and then jerks back up when he wakes. In a heroin user, this can be a warning of excess sedation from using too much. "Being on the nod is the first baby step on a slippery slope toward overdosing,"[33] says Ciccarone.

The Perils of Prolonged Heroin Use

People who use heroin for a prolonged period of time (that is, those who are addicted) will invariably experience a marked decline in their overall health. Repeated heroin use by men has been associated with sexual dysfunction. Among women, heroin use can cause irregular menstrual cycles and miscarriages if they become pregnant while using the drug. Severe stomach cramps, chronic constipation, and inability to sleep are all common among regular heroin users. Also, heroin can contribute to weakened immune systems, putting users at risk for contracting many types of disease.

Scientists have long known about a close connection between prolonged heroin use and deadly infectious diseases such as HIV/AIDS and various forms of hepatitis (inflammation of the liver).

A 2019 CDC analysis showed that hepatitis A cases surged by nearly 300 percent between 2016 and 2018, and a large number of those cases were among drug users. Sharing a needle that has been used by someone with an infectious disease is the main culprit in the spread of disease among heroin users. As NIDA explains, "Sharing of injection equipment or fluids can lead to some of the most severe consequences of heroin use—infections with hepatitis B and C, HIV, and a host of other blood-borne viruses, which drug users can then pass on to their sexual partners and children."[34]

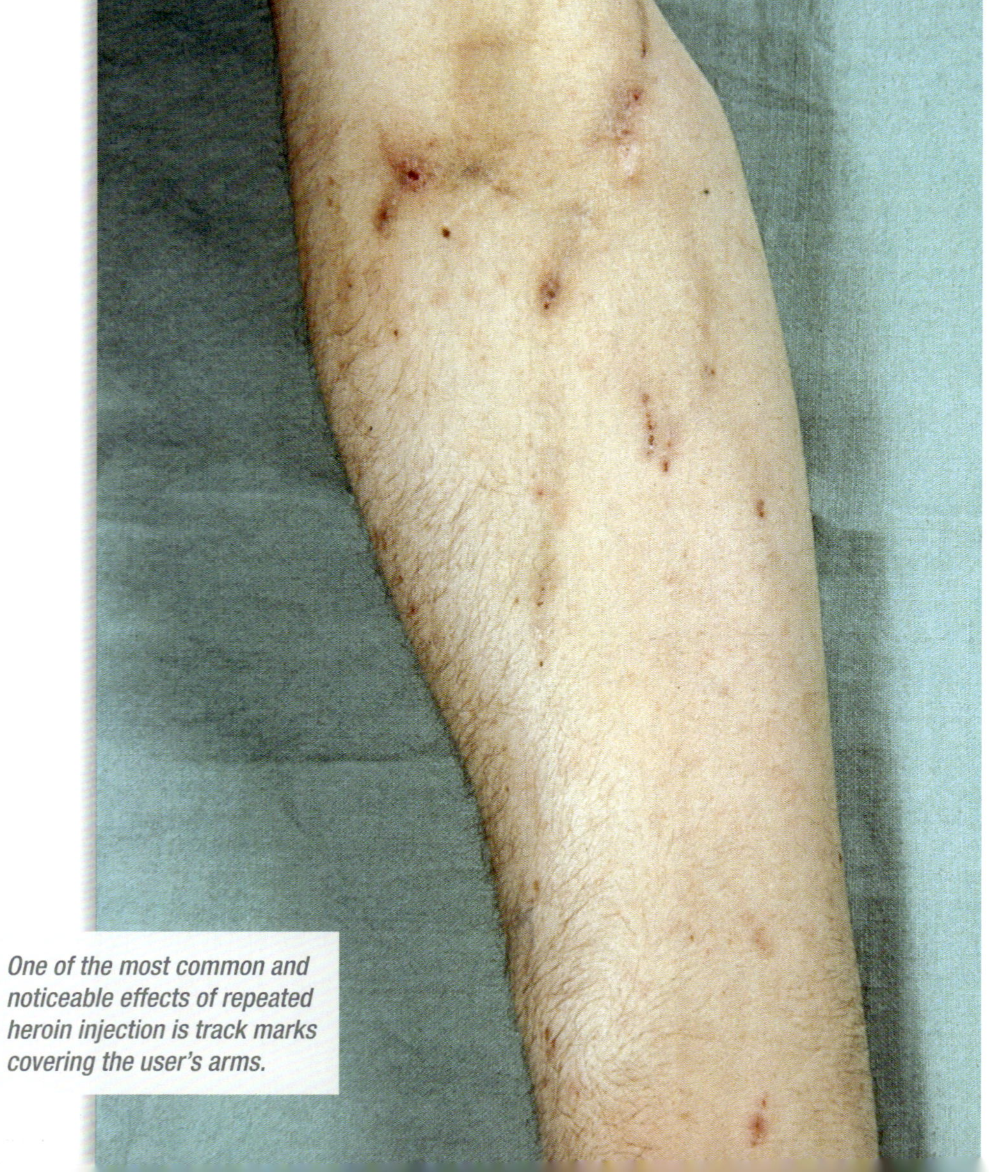

One of the most common and noticeable effects of repeated heroin injection is track marks covering the user's arms.

One particularly dangerous risk for longtime heroin users is infection of the heart lining and valves, which is known as infective endocarditis. The condition develops when contaminated needles introduce harmful bacteria into the bloodstream, and the bacteria build up on the heart's valves or its inside lining. According to a 2019 study by Ohio State University researchers, hospital admissions for infectious endocarditis related to intravenous drug use increased by more than 400 percent between 2012 and 2017 at the university's Wexner Medical Center. Cardiologist Serena Day, who was lead author of the study, notes that the drastic increase in infective endocarditis happened concurrently with the soaring prevalence of heroin addiction. "What's most striking is how quickly this problem got out of hand," says Day. "Five years ago, this disease was very uncommon for us. Now, it's become so common that we can't keep up."[35]

The bacteria from contaminated needles that causes infective endocarditis can lead to other problems as well, such as abscesses, or boils, on the skin. These are badly infected sites that become red, painful, and pus-filled. According to Ken Seeley, an addiction specialist and treatment counselor, contaminated needles deliver the bacteria past the skin barrier into the bloodstream and soft tissues. As Seeley explains,

> Multiple punctures in the same area may worsen the wound and will, in turn, be more likely to be infected during the heroin injections. Forming a skin abscess from injecting heroin becomes common during the constant urge to get another fix. Multiple boils may form as the addict searches for new injection points that aren't collecting fluid and swelling with pain, redness, and warmth.[36]

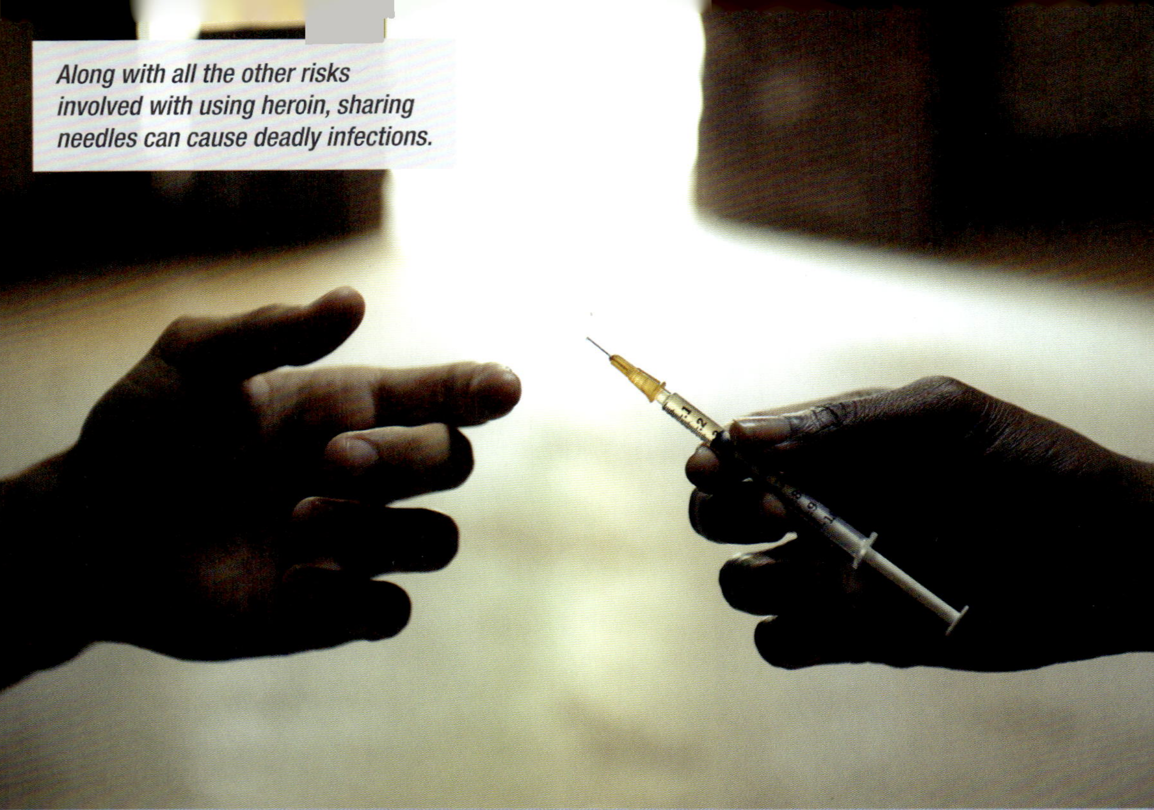

Although abscesses may not sound as serious as other conditions caused by heroin injections, they have the potential to become life threatening. If left untreated, the infection from a skin abscess can poison the blood and spread throughout the body—a dangerous condition called sepsis. The infection can also cause the life-threatening condition gangrene, which is the death of soft tissue from loss of blood supply.

Sniffing and Smoking Heroin

When thinking about the worst health risks associated with heroin, people may think only of injecting the drug. But no one should consider snorting or smoking heroin to be less risky—consuming heroin is never risk free, no matter how someone uses it. Those who repeatedly snort it, for instance, can damage their nasal mucous membrane, which is the protective tissue that lines the cavity inside the nose. Snorting heroin can also cause a hole to form in the roof of the mouth and the nasal septum, which is the bony formation that separates the nasal passages. This can lead to chronic nosebleeds and, in severe cases, can result in permanent damage.

Users who smoke heroin, which is known by the slang term *chasing the dragon*, are also seriously risking their health. The drug can take a heavy toll on the lungs, markedly raising the risk for lung diseases such as pneumonia, chronic obstructive pulmonary disease (COPD), and tuberculosis as well as conditions such as chronic coughing and asthma. According to Daniel Ciccarone, heroin smoking is not common in the United States, but it is common in Europe. In 2019 a team of researchers from Liverpool, England, published a study about the harms associated with heroin smoking. In their final report, they write, "In a population of heroin smokers, we found a high burden of lung disease."[37]

Brain Damage

Whether people smoke, snort, or inject heroin, they are putting their brains at risk. According to NIDA, prolonged heroin use changes the physical structure of the brain, which can lead to many problems, including mental illness. Long-term users may develop mental disorders such as depression and antisocial personality disorder. And in users who already suffer from depression, heroin use can worsen symptoms. This can result in everything from anxiety and nervousness to suicidal thoughts.

In some cases, severe heroin use has resulted in severe, crippling brain damage. One of the effects of heroin is slowed breathing; if breathing is severely slowed, it can lead to coma and permanent brain damage. Also, heroin can prevent the brain from receiving enough oxygen, which is a condition called hypoxia. When the brain is starved of oxygen, the brain cells begin to die, sometimes within thirty seconds of losing their oxygen supply. If enough brain cells die, the inevitable result is the death of the person who used the heroin.

The amount of brain damage an overdose can cause depends on how long the brain is deprived of oxygen, without which it cannot survive. Some overdose victims recover fully because their brain was not without oxygen long enough for the brain cells to die. But others are not so fortunate. The Foundation for a Drug-Free World recounts the story of a twenty-one-year-old man named Jim, who was out with his friends when one offered him some heroin. Jim had already tried the drug a few times, so he accepted the offer and snorted the line of heroin. Fifteen minutes later Jim passed out, and then he fell into a deep coma—which lasted for more than two months. "Today," says the foundation, "he is confined to a wheelchair, unable to write, barely able to read. Whatever dreams and aspirations he once had are gone."[38]

Some people who have survived such serious incidents have wound up needing life support and caregiver assistance for the rest of their lives. "Having your body go without oxygen can result in damage to all parts of the body," explains Sarah Wakeman, the medical director of the Substance Use Disorders Initiative and the Addiction Consult Team at Massachusetts General Hospital. "That can range from a minor deficit all the way to people being in permanent vegetative states. Some of these complications are similar to imagining someone who has had a massive stroke."[39]

A Devastating Condition

What happens after an overdose can be just as dangerous as the overdose itself. Consider that someone who overdoses often crumples to the ground. If the person lies immobile for a long period of time, and is positioned in such a way that circulation is cut off to the limbs, this can result in a condition known as rhabdomyolysis (or rhabdo, for short). Wakeman explains: "The pressure on that part of the body literally causes the muscles to start to break down."[40] This can lead to kidney failure as these organs are overwhelmed trying to filter out damaging by-products of muscle breakdown moving through the bloodstream.

Some overdose survivors who developed rhabdo have had to have a limb or part of a limb amputated after it was trapped beneath them while they were unconscious. The limb went without blood circulation for so long that the tissues began to die. This happened to Jared, a young man in his twenties from Tennessee who overdosed on heroin and prescription opioids in April 2016. All Jared remembers about that time is sitting down on a stairway to smoke a cigarette, and beyond that his memory is blank. "I nodded out,"[41] he says. His body bent over and his upper half fell between his legs, completely cutting off circulation to his lower body. By the time someone found him, Jared was in a coma and his lower body had been without circulation for up to ten hours. At the hospital, he remained on life support for weeks. Because of the circulation loss to his lower body, both of his legs had to be amputated.

The Ultimate Danger

People who use heroin have a very high risk of dying from overdose. Every day, reports the CDC, an average of 130 Americans die from an overdose of heroin or other opioids. And according to a study published in February 2020 in the *Journal of the American Medical Association*, deaths from heroin overdoses have risen sharply in the past two decades. The seventeen-year longitudinal study, which was conducted by researchers from the Substance Abuse and Mental Health Services Administration (SAMHSA) and the National Institutes of Health, involved a national survey of eight hundred thousand adults aged eighteen and older. The study revealed that overdose deaths involving heroin soared to more than fifteen thousand in 2018 from just under twenty-one hundred in 2002—an increase of more than 600 percent.

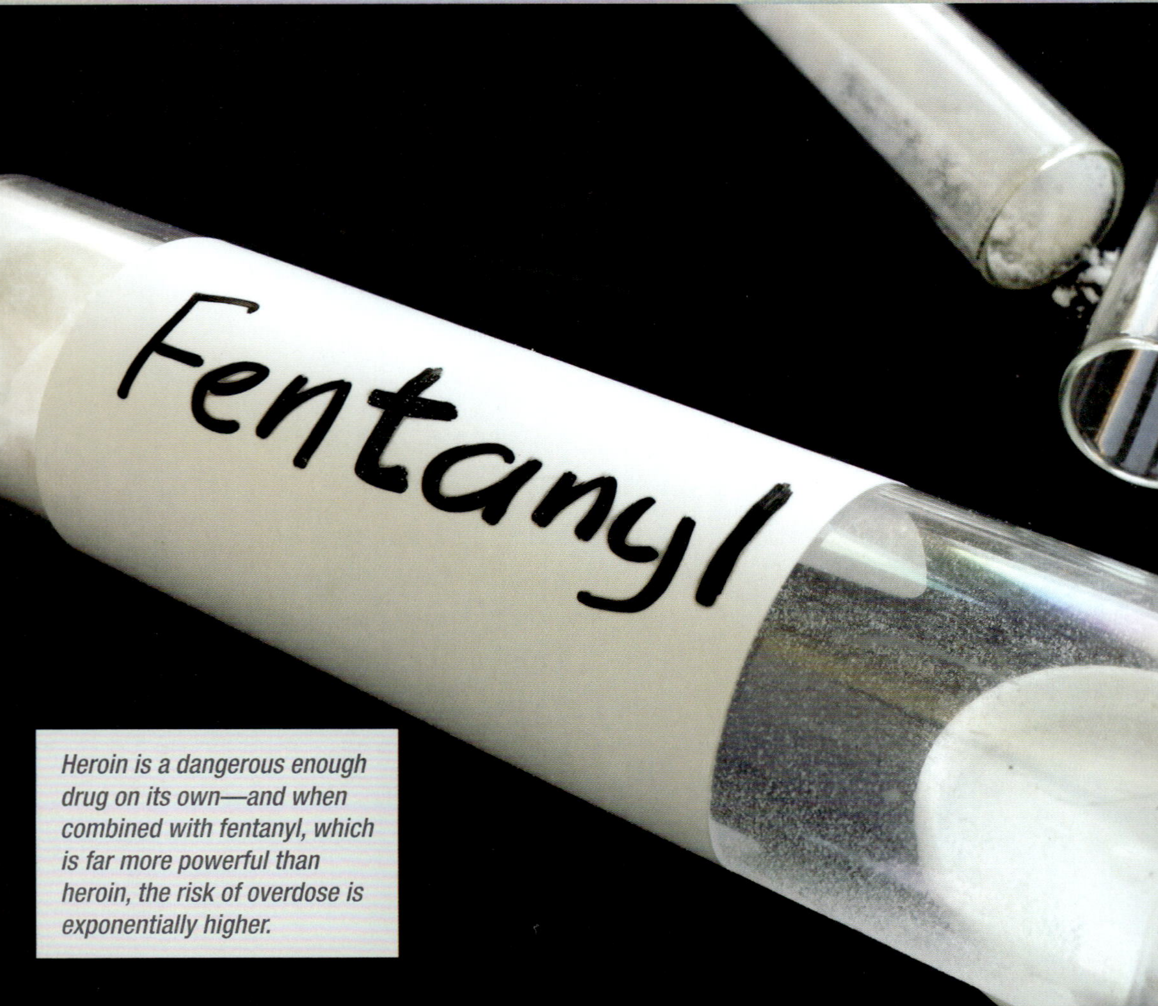

Heroin is a dangerous enough drug on its own—and when combined with fentanyl, which is far more powerful than heroin, the risk of overdose is exponentially higher.

The risk of a heroin overdose causing a person to stop breathing is even greater if the heroin has been mixed with fentanyl—and this is happening with alarming regularity. "Many dealers now lace heroin with fentanyl, a painkiller that is much stronger than heroin and can cause an overdose more quickly,"[42] explains physician Steven Dowshen.

Overdose symptoms include slow and shallow breathing, clammy skin, and even convulsions. The lips and fingernails of overdose victims may turn blue or purplish—a sign that their bodies are being starved of oxygen. They may be unconscious or unresponsive, or they may be awake but unable to speak. Overdose victims may vomit, choke, or make gurgling sounds. They may even make a sound that others may mistake for ordinary snoring—which can lead to deadly consequences. As the Foundations Recovery Network, an addiction treatment center, explains,

> There are cases of overdose where people involved think that the overdosed person is fine because he begins to snore. This activity may be deemed "sleeping it off" but that interpretation can be dead wrong. It is critical not to ignore snoring, even if the person is a known snorer, or gurgling. Snoring can be an indication of breathing trouble, and any obstruction of the breathing airways can be fatal.[43]

Twenty-year-old Landon Biggers died from a heroin overdose on November 21, 2017. That morning his older sister, Brittaney, watched in horror as their father tried to revive Landon while they waited for the ambulance. But by the time the paramedics got there, it was too late—Landon had already died. His death devastated his family. Because he overdosed on the floor of Brittaney's bedroom, she could not stand to go in there, even to get clothes from her closet. Everywhere she looked, she remembered her little brother lying on the floor, dying. "My house makes me sick," Brittaney says. "It's so quiet here now, I can physically feel his absence. It's like silence that slaps you in the face."[44]

Heroin Kills

Although not everyone who overdoses on heroin dies, people flirt with death every time they use it. Using heroin also carries innumerable health risks, from lung diseases to deadly heart

A Gruesome Way to Die

No matter how they put heroin into their bodies, people who use it are gambling with their health and their lives. Those who inject it are taking the biggest risk of all because of the many dangers associated with needles. And that risk is compounded when heroin addicts use black tar heroin, which is made in Mexico and is so-named because it is sticky, like roofing tar. It is cheaper to produce than powdered heroin and is therefore cheaper for users to buy, but the lower price is because black tar heroin is made with crude processing methods and contains impurities that make it especially dangerous.

Between October 2 and November 24, 2019, seven people in San Diego, California, died after injecting black tar heroin. The cause of death was a horrific bacterial infection called myonecrosis, which is also known as flesh-eating bacteria because of how it "eats" (meaning destroys) muscle tissue. When people contract myonecrosis, it spreads rapidly throughout the body and often leads to death. Those who survive may suffer from permanent organ damage and/or need to have limbs amputated to stop the spread of infection. San Diego health officials say they have never seen an outbreak of myonecrosis as severe as this one. "It's just another situation where it shows the dangerous epidemic of the opioids we're facing now," says Dr. Paul Little, the medical director of an addiction treatment center in Southern California.

Quoted in Michael Levenson, "7 Heroin Users Die from Flesh-Eating Bacteria in San Diego," *New York Times*, December 5, 2019. www.nytimes.com.

damage to hepatitis and AIDS to severe, permanent brain damage. No one can tell this terrible story better than chronic heroin users like Allie from Atlanta. Because of what heroin has done to her health and well-being, she hates to see young people get hooked on it. She tries to scare them away from using the drug—but she still sells it to them to help support her own habit. Allie cried openly as she explained this during an interview with CNN reporters. "All these kids come around and it breaks my heart," she says. "Believe it or not, I tell them, 'Honey, this is not what you want to do. It's the end of the line. . . . It's gonna kill you."[45]

—Allie, a heroin addict from Atlanta, Georgia

CHAPTER FOUR

The Challenges of Treatment and Recovery

People who are addicted to heroin face tough challenges when they decide to stop using. Few are able to give up the drug without treatment, and that is largely because they fear the horrors of withdrawal. Addiction specialist Marc Myer says that the mental withdrawal is one of the worst parts of getting off any opioid. He describes it as a combination of "severe depression and feeling that you're never going to pull out of that state." According to Myer, it is well known among addiction treatment specialists that because of those feelings of hopelessness, "the anticipation of the withdrawal is oftentimes worse than the actual thing."[46]

A Courageous Decision

Many people who are addicted to heroin know they have a problem, but they have no idea where to turn for help. They may try to give up the drug on their own but find the process excruciating and end up right back where they were. This was true for twenty-two-year-old Abbey Zorzi. When she was a sophomore in high school, she received a prescription for Vicodin after having her wisdom teeth removed. She quickly became addicted and was soon buying pills on the street. When she could no longer get them, she switched to injecting heroin.

After just a week or two of using heroin, Zorzi felt "trapped and scared" and had a sick feeling that there was no turning back. "Heroin had total control over my life, physically and mentally," she says. "Once that drug was in me, it told me what to do. I didn't take heroin; heroin took me."[47] Zorski knew she had to stop using the drug, and she wanted to stop using, but she did not know how. She tried quitting on her own numerous times, but she never succeeded. She explains:

> This dark time lasted for about two years. I went from being a star athlete to a heroin junkie. I pleaded with myself and cried on a daily basis because I wanted to stop using, but my addiction would not allow me to stop. My hatred for myself was so strong and deep. Every day was dark and morbid in my world. My life began to slip away right before my eyes. I have never experienced a more desperate and hopeless feeling than when I sat on the cold, hard bathroom floor getting ready to use once again.[48]

Zorzi finally worked up the courage to seek treatment during her freshman year in college. She says it was the hardest decision she has ever made. She went to a rehab facility where the medical staff helped her detox by giving her medication to ease the pain of withdrawal. "They left their doors open all day in case I needed to talk," she says. "They listened to me and comforted me while I blurted out all of my problems."[49]

How long addiction treatment lasts depends on the severity of the person's addiction. Zorzi's stay in a rehab facility lasted for a month. Today she considers herself to be in recovery from her heroin addiction. She continues to attend support group meetings,

Many heroin treatment programs involve different types of therapy, such as group therapy or support groups.

and she visits schools, prevention programs, juvenile detention centers, jails, and mental hospitals to give motivational speeches about her recovery. She asks, "What good is recovery if I am not speaking out and helping others?"[50]

Stigma and Other Barriers to Treatment

Zorzi is one of the fortunate few who have received treatment for heroin addiction. Despite the devastating consequences, and the spike in overdose deaths, only a small percentage of those who need treatment are ever treated. Often, it is because they are ashamed of their addiction. "Drug addiction is a highly stigmatized disease," says Zorzi. "Many victims of the disease remain silent because they feel guilty, embarrassed, confused, or powerless."[51]

In addition to the stigma, a huge barrier to treatment is that it is expensive—prohibitively

44

so for many, perhaps even most, who suffer from heroin addiction. Health insurance (if patients even have it) does not always cover addiction treatment. Even if it does, insurance often covers only a portion of what treatment costs. There is usually a lifetime cap on benefits as well as copays and deductibles that make out-of-pocket costs extremely steep.

Inpatient care often costs tens of thousands of dollars, far more than most people can afford. One example is Serenity, an inpatient and detox facility near Denver, Colorado, where a four-week program costs more than $15,000 *per day*. The facility accepts private insurance and offers some financial assistance. But under federal law, facilities like Serenity are barred from accepting Medicaid, or government assistance with medical expenses for people with limited incomes.

Another major barrier to treatment is the often overwhelming process of finding help in the first place. Unless physicians are trained in addiction medicine, most are not qualified to diagnose or treat patients who are addicted to heroin. Compounding this is that there is no reliable, credible directory of facilities to help people find an accredited and effective treatment program. "We haven't come as far in providing treatment as we need to," admits Dr. Lawrence Brown Jr., an addiction treatment specialist. "It's not always easy to find an accredited program in your area. It's changing, but not fast enough."[52]

Mary Early knows firsthand how hard it is to find a quality addiction treatment program. Like so many others, the thirty-two-year-old from Lexington, Kentucky, became addicted to heroin after using prescription painkillers. When Early decided to seek help, she spent three months making telephone calls to about twenty clinics that either did not have space for her or did not accept Medicaid insurance. "It's frustrating," Early wrote in response to a *Politico* survey of people affected by the opioid crisis. "I need help now. I'm trying not to die right now."[53]

—Mary Early, a woman from Lexington, Kentucky, who could not find affordable treatment for her heroin addiction

Tough to Treat

Even for those who seek treatment, heroin addiction is notoriously difficult to treat. One reason is brain chemistry: because repeated heroin use alters the way the brain works, it must be retrained to function normally—which can take a very long time. "My brain felt like it was rewired," says former addict Jim Pietrowski. "My body, mind and soul. It's a day at a time."[54] Every patient is different, and how much time it takes to recover varies from one person to another. Addiction experts say it can take from six months to a decade, or even longer.

The high likelihood of relapse is another major reason why heroin addiction is so tough to treat. Severe cravings and withdrawal can seem impossible to overcome, sending addicts right back to the drug. Twenty-nine-year-old Jasmine Johnson, a former heroin addict, can attest to this. "A lot of times in your addiction, things are getting better," says Johnson. "You see a light at the end of the tunnel. And it ends up being the freight train

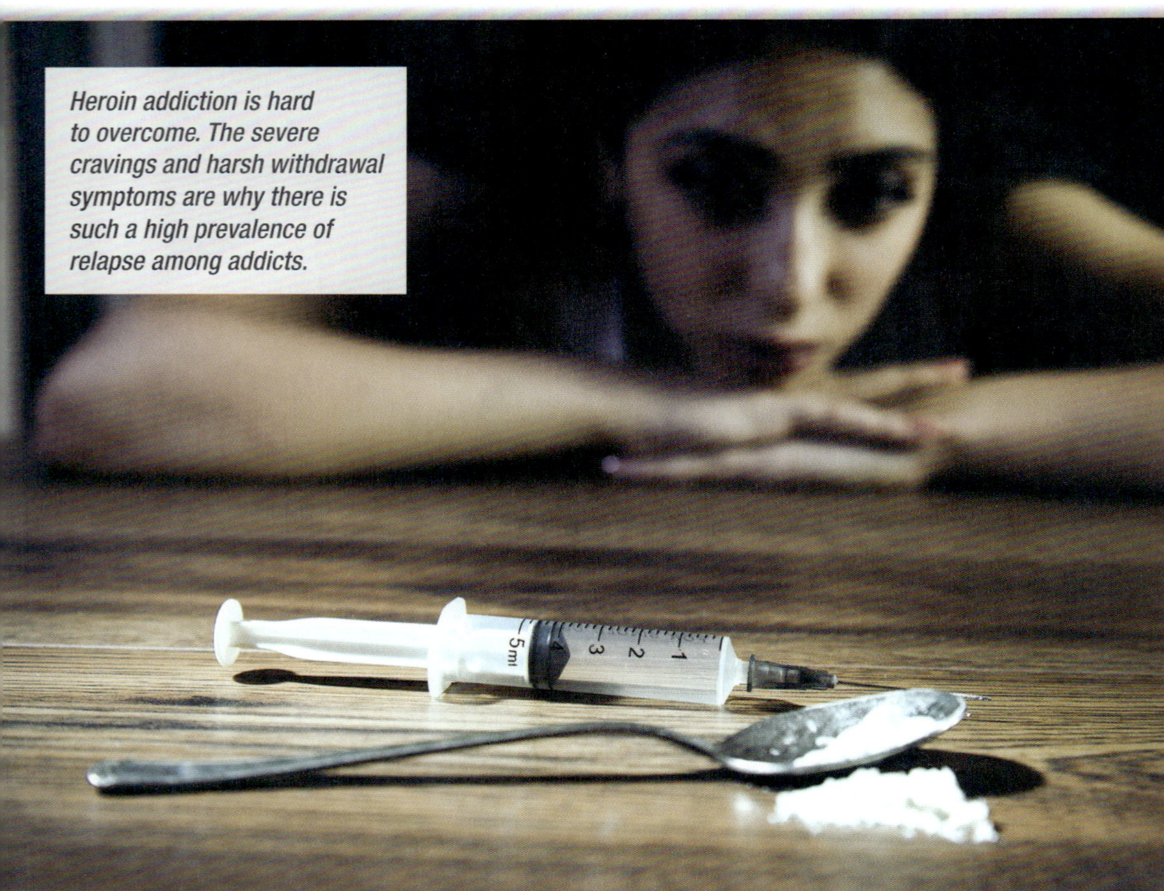

Heroin addiction is hard to overcome. The severe cravings and harsh withdrawal symptoms are why there is such a high prevalence of relapse among addicts.

coming at you."[55] It is not at all uncommon for heroin addicts to relapse four, five, or even more times before they finally beat their addiction.

The Gold Standard

Addiction experts widely agree that the best approach to treating heroin addiction is medication-assisted treatment, or MAT. This approach, often called the gold standard of addiction treatment, includes a combination of addiction counseling and prescription medications. Because of its high record of success, addiction experts and health officials overwhelmingly support the MAT approach. One supporter is Elinore F. McCance-Katz, a physician who serves as the assistant secretary for mental health and substance use at the US Department of Health and Human Services. She writes, "There is strong scientific evidence that this combination of therapeutic interventions is life-saving and can enable people to recover to healthy lives."[56]

With MAT, patients under medical supervision take drugs like buprenorphine, methadone, and naltrexone, which can greatly reduce cravings and withdrawal symptoms without causing the high that comes with heroin use. Addiction specialists decide which medication to prescribe according to each patient's level of addiction and individual needs. For Emilie Cote, who started using drugs as a teen and later became addicted to heroin, buprenorphine was crucial to recovery. She says it gave her "enough

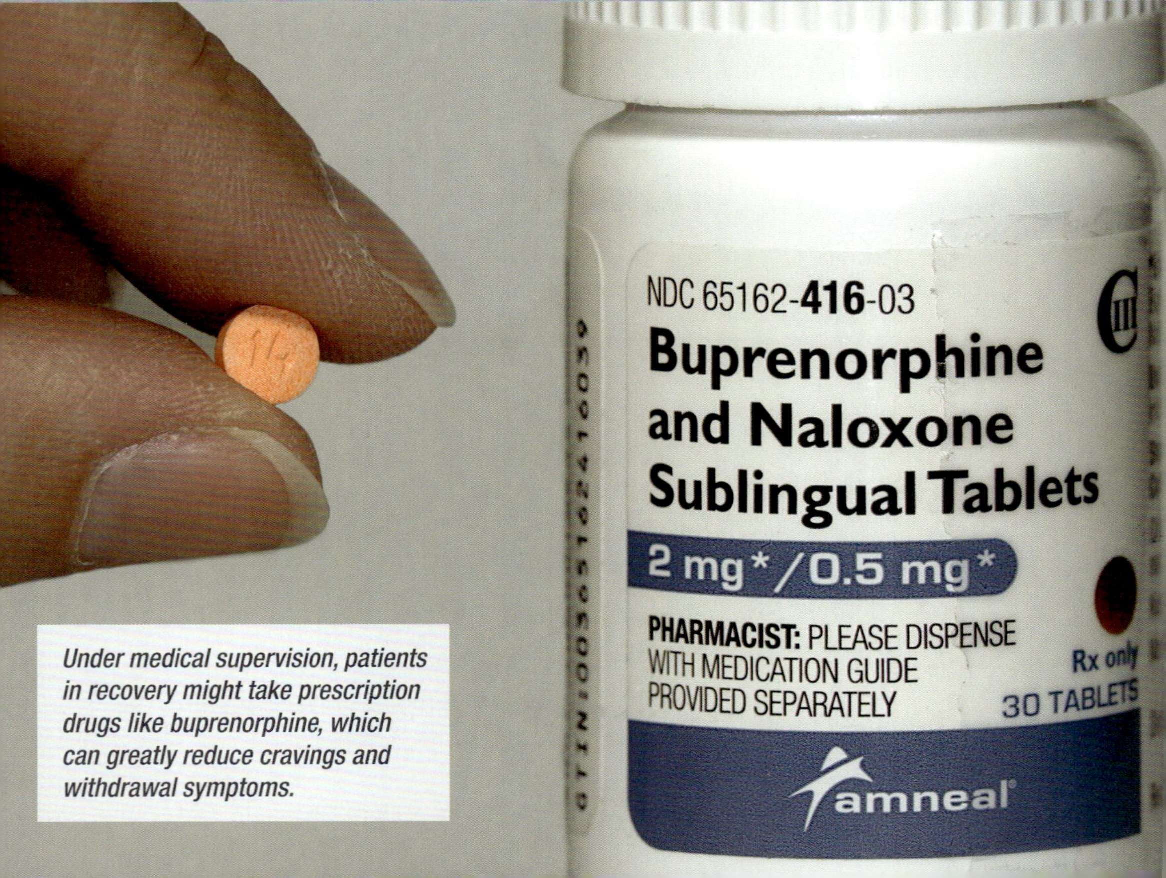

Under medical supervision, patients in recovery might take prescription drugs like buprenorphine, which can greatly reduce cravings and withdrawal symptoms.

time away from the euphoria that you get from heroin. . . . I felt like I could rebuild my life without absolutely needing that feeling."[57]

Methadone and buprenorphine are opioids, but the brain responds differently to them than it does to heroin and other opioids. Methadone and buprenorphine activate the same receptors as neurotransmitters (and opioid drugs), but it takes longer for them to be absorbed into the blood. This not only lessens withdrawal symptoms but also breaks the psychological link between using a drug and immediately feeling high from it. Methadone and buprenorphine are both available by prescription, but under federal law, methadone may only be distributed by clinics that are certified by SAMHSA.

Unlike methadone and buprenorphine, naltrexone is not an opioid. It is a narcotic blocker, or a nonopioid drug that is known as an opioid antagonist. Naltrexone binds to opioid receptors and blocks them from being activated by other opioids. So if a patient who is taking naltrexone uses heroin, they will not get high. In other words, naltrexone eliminates the reward of getting high, which in turn reduces the person's desire for heroin.

Behavioral Therapies

Along with treating heroin addiction with medications, addiction experts also recommend one or more types of behavioral or psychological therapy. This is important for recovering addicts who are not only suffering from the physical aspects of drug addiction but also from lingering psychological issues. Journalist Francie Diep has interviewed dozens of addicts over the years for stories about addiction, and she says they often told her how important such therapy was in fighting their addiction. "Some have trauma to process," says Diep. "Even without a tough childhood, just spending a lot of time using can expose people to something akin to a quiet, domestic war."[58]

Several behavioral therapy approaches have proved to be successful, especially when used in combination with MAT. Behavioral approaches to therapy center on giving people incentives to stay off heroin, modifying their behaviors and attitudes related to the drug, and increasing skills in coping with life stressors. Two of the most successful approaches are contingency management (CM) and cognitive behavioral therapy (CBT).

The CM approach employs a voucher-based system wherein patients can earn "points" for every drug-free urine sample they provide. They can then exchange these points for items that encourage a drug-free lifestyle, such as movie passes or healthy food items. The point values start out small but increase as the number of drug-free tests increases. A positive drug test, indicating that a patient has used again, will reset the point value back to the low beginning value. Another form of CM uses chances to win cash prizes instead of awarding points. Participants who provide a drug-free urine sample get to draw from a bowl for the chance to win a prize worth between $1 and $100. Participants in CM can also be rewarded points or chances to win cash based on attending counseling sessions or completing goals. When used in combination with MAT, CM has been shown to be highly effective in helping patients stay in treatment and off opioids.

The CBT approach helps recovering addicts identify the connection between their thoughts, feelings, and actions and understand how these affect their recovery. When people understand why they feel or act in a certain way, and especially how their feelings and actions lead them to use heroin, they are better able to beat their addiction. A main focus of CBT is on helping recovering addicts identify distorted thinking and negative "automatic thoughts," which often stem from misperceptions and feelings of anxiety or self-doubt. Many addicts have turned to heroin in an attempt to cope with these negative thoughts and feelings, so understanding what is at the root of their behavior is essential. So is understanding which situations will trigger their drug use and learning positive ways to deal with these triggers.

There are several CBT techniques. One of these, called thought records, requires recovering addicts to explore their negative thoughts and look for objective evidence that will refute them. The goal of this exercise is to help patients learn to have more realistic and less harsh thoughts by examining what they are thinking. Another CBT technique is imagery-based exposure, which has patients recall a memory that elicits strong negative feelings for them. Patients pay attention to the sights, sounds, thoughts, and feelings surrounding the memory. The idea behind this technique is to reduce the anxiety associated with such memories by frequently revisiting them, thereby diminishing their impact on the person. The pleasant activity schedule is another common CBT technique, whereby recovering addicts come up with a weekly list of enjoyable and healthy activities that are easy to perform. Having such a schedule helps addicts reduce their negative automatic thoughts and control their need to use heroin.

Questionable Treatment Methods

Not all treatment methods for heroin addiction are created equal. This was revealed during a 2019 in-depth investigation by the news and opinion media group Vox, which uncovered some troubling information about treatment centers in the United States. These facilities are not required to have trained doctors or nurses on staff—and most do not. About 70 percent use the 12-step method, which was pioneered by Alcoholics Anonymous in 1953. Although some claim it is effective for those who are trying to recover from alcoholism, it has not proved to be effective for treating narcotic addiction. And most of the facilities that use the 12-step method do not believe in using MAT, claiming that it just substitutes one drug for another—a point of view that addiction experts say is antiquated, dangerous, and proved wrong.

Another finding from the Vox investigation was that these facilities typically kick people out for relapsing—which, according to addiction specialist Sarah Wakeman, is cruel as well as ineffective. "If you were in the hospital for a heart attack and you had another heart attack, we wouldn't discharge you from care," says Wakeman. "We would intensify your care and think what more we need to do medically."[59]

As prevalent as heroin addiction has become in recent years, there is a vast and growing need for treatment. Yet there are major problems with (and obstacles to) effective, qualified treatment programs. "There has never been a system that demands quality of care for treatment of substance use disorders," says Nora Volkow, the director of NIDA. "Programs have not had any incentive to actually change their practices or improve what they are doing."[60]

People who are addicted to heroin can be treated and do recover from their addiction. Unfortunately, however, most are never treated. The reasons for this range from the fear of withdrawal to the lack of a centralized database of credible rehabilitation facilities to treatment options whose cost is simply out of reach for the average person. It is not unusual for people to spend months desperately trying to get help—a wait that may, tragically, prove to be too long for many.

CHAPTER FIVE

Stopping Heroin Addiction Before It Starts

Heroin is a dangerous and addictive drug, with extraordinarily high relapse rates. As essential as effective treatments are in the fight against heroin and other opioids in the United States, even more important are preventive strategies—methods of dissuading people from using these drugs in the first place. This is especially crucial for young people. Their brains are not yet fully developed, which makes them more vulnerable to addiction than adults. In fact, research has shown that about 90 percent of addictions start during the teenage years.

Research has also revealed that of teenage heroin users, an overwhelming majority were hooked on prescription painkillers before getting addicted to heroin. Thus, drug prevention programs at the community level or in schools typically focus on all opioid drugs rather than singling out heroin. In a June 2019 blog post, NIDA director Nora Volkow wrote about the importance of such programs. "It is not enough to focus all our resources on treating people who are already addicted to opioids," she said. "Keeping people who do not have an opioid use disorder from becoming addicted is an equally important task."[61]

A Controversial Tactic

One effort to prevent young people from using drugs has been embroiled in controversy: student drug testing programs at middle schools and high schools throughout the United States. According to an August 2017 survey conducted by the US Department of Health and Human Services and the CDC, 38 percent of schools had drug testing programs in place as of 2016 (the most recent year for which national figures are available).

Two school districts that have implemented drug testing are the Fort Scott Unified School District in Fort Scott, Kansas, and the Bushland Independent School District near Amarillo, Texas. In Fort Scott, if students test positive, they are suspended from extracurricular activities, but they also are eligible for drug treatment through a partnership with a mental health provider. In Amarillo, superintendent of schools Chris Wigington says that drug testing has proved effective in helping students resist peer pressure to take drugs. "We all know peer pressure is very real,"[62] he says.

In January 2020, a high school in Plainwell, Michigan, enacted a drug testing program for student athletes—and as with all such programs, reactions were mixed. Some students and parents have spoken out against it, but others wholeheartedly support it. One Plainwell student who agreed to speak anonymously said that as soon as the program took effect, he could see that it was working. "The benefits are already being shown," he says, "as I can see some of my peers cutting down on use of the drugs they are testing for." The teen added a cautionary note, however: "The negative side of this is the kids that all they have is sports in life might be swayed away from playing if they know they can't stay clean."[63]

Evidence on the impact of school drug testing is inconclusive. For example, NIDA has found that random testing has little to no impact on short-term drug use for student athletes, but long-term drug use seems to be reduced. And according to the American Civil Liberties Union (ACLU), "There is no concrete evidence that randomly drug testing students deters drug use. And it does not address the reasons why kids turn to drugs in the first place."[64]

Due to the lack of overwhelming evidence on the efficacy of random drug testing in schools, organizations like the American Academy of Pediatrics, the National Education Association, and the American Academy of Child & Adolescent Psychiatry are opposed to the practice. According to the American Academy of

One preventive measure adopted by a number of high schools is drug testing for student athletes. It is a controversial practice, though, and there is little evidence that it actually deters drug use.

Pediatrics, drug testing harbors "the potential for breach of privacy" (such as when a student's legitimate prescription medications show up on a drug test) and "detrimental consequences"[65] (such as students whose drug tests are positive being suspended from school, an increased school dropout rate among students who fear they would fail a drug test, and/or the increased use of drugs that are not easily detectable on a drug screen).

Project HOPE

Random drug testing is one of many preventive strategies that schools are using to try and cut down on heroin and other drug use. Another is the Heroin and Opioid Prevention Education (HOPE) program, which grew out of the escalating opioid abuse problem in communities throughout Pennsylvania. Students, teachers, and administrators who participate in the program learn what heroin and other opioids are; the signs and symptoms of opioid abuse; how opioid use affects health, relationships, and life; local resources; and where to go for help. The program's webpage even offers a resource for people to obtain training to use naloxone, a drug that can help reverse the effects of an overdose. HOPE has proved to be so effective in Pennsylvania that other states have adopted it as well, including Alaska, Oregon, and Ohio.

Ohio state officials have been searching for effective drug prevention programs for a number of years. The small town of Belpre, Ohio, experienced great tragedy in 2015 when a popular high school athlete died of an overdose just before his senior year. In response, the school decided to implement its own HOPE curriculum. The program is part of a larger statewide effort to prevent substance abuse. Lessons designed to develop and shape students' knowledge, attitudes, and skills about drug prevention are taught at all grade levels as part of a school's health education classes. In one program, fourth-grade students engage in a role-playing exercise in which they learn to stand up for themselves and refuse drugs.

The program appears to be working. As of late 2019, there had been no overdose deaths of school-age children since the athlete's overdose in 2015. And one Belpre assistant principal notes that "the 20-minute lessons are developmentally appropriate" and "easy to implement."[66]

As well received as the program has been, it is also somewhat controversial. One reason is that it begins in kindergarten, where safety education has traditionally focused on issues such as "stranger danger" and avoiding household hazards. Drug education typically does not begin until students are a little older. But teachers following the HOPE curriculum are encouraged to discuss real-life situations, such as being pressured to try drugs, even with younger students. Ohio's attorney general, Mike DeWine, emphasizes the importance of starting prevention initiatives as early as possible: "What makes us think we can wait until the fourth or fifth [grade] to do something about the drug problem? If this is as important as I think it is, we need to get serious about it."[67]

Some drug prevention programs begin as early as kindergarten. Supporters say that children are better prepared to turn away from drug use as teens if they learn about the risks at a very young age.

Located on Maryland's Eastern Shore, Queen Anne's County is a beautiful, picturesque region—and one that is plagued by some of the country's highest opioid overdose rates. "We have a serious problem here," says Eric B. Johnson, the county's emergency management director. He and other residents could see the problem all around them, from family members who had died of overdose to students overheard on a school bus talking about how good heroin is. The group knew they needed to do something, and during the fall of 2019, they came up with a plan: to create a huge haunted house that would open on Halloween. This would, however, be no ordinary haunted house. Rather than encountering shrieking, screeching ghosts and witches, visitors would take a journey through the nightmare of drug addiction.

It was known as the Haunted Trap House and featured highly realistic scenes with teen actors. The scenes included a drug den, a drug-related arrest, a court hearing, a jail cell, a traumatic family crisis, and a disturbing overdose. Visitors saw for themselves the horrific details of someone shooting up heroin. They heard screams and grief-stricken sobbing. And when their tour came to an end, they had seen, felt, and experienced the horrors of drug addiction as closely as they ever could without putting a needle in their own arm. "If we can help one person, just one person stops using or doesn't start using because of this," says Johnson, "it's all worth it."

Quoted in Petula Dvorak, "This Town Turned Its Opioid Nightmare into a Haunted House: And It's Terrifying," *Washington Post*, October 21, 2019. www.washingtonpost.com.

More than Just Law Enforcement

Law enforcement agencies are also playing an important role in drug prevention. Although the DEA is best known for the law enforcement aspect of its work, its activities go far beyond that. The agency also provides free drug prevention education materials and programs to educators, community leaders, parents, and the public. Programs offered by the DEA include Just Think Twice and Get Smart About Drugs. Another is Operation Prevention, which aims to educate students about the impact of opioid abuse so they can talk about the issue both in the classroom and at home. Resources are available for elementary, middle, and high schools to use as part of their instruction. These include digital lessons on topics such as how medications work in the body, a video on how to start a classroom conversation on drugs, and an e-learning module on the science behind addiction.

One of the most effective aspects of Operation Prevention is its virtual field trips, which allow students to "meet" people who have struggled with addiction. These include videos that feature real-life stories from recovering addicts and family members who have been affected by addiction. The virtual field trips are supplemented by companion activities that help jump-start classroom conversations. One activity features two retired profes-

Now-retired professional football players Lyle Sendlein (left) and Levi Brown (right) of the Arizona Cardinals face off at training camp in 2007. Both players were frequently prescribed opioids for injuries they sustained while playing football. Both men are part of Operation Prevention, which aims to educate students about the impact of opioid abuse.

sional football players: Levi Brown and Lyle Sendlein, who were frequently prescribed opioids for injuries they sustained while playing football. In their video, Brown and Sendlein explain some of the risks of taking opioids and encourage young athletes to learn about alternative (nondrug) ways to manage pain.

Through its Campus Drug Prevention program, the DEA extends its prevention efforts onto college campuses. Program features include a podcast, news and research articles, and information about upcoming events. On its website, the DEA talks about drug misuse on campus as well as ways students can help friends who are struggling with addiction. "It's difficult to have a conversation with someone on campus you suspect might have a drug problem," the Campus Drug Prevention website notes, "especially if it is someone you have a close relationship with, such as a roommate, teammate, classmate, or coworker. And yet as hard as that discussion may be, it may go a long way toward helping someone in need."[68]

CDC Prevention Efforts

Like the DEA, the CDC is an agency of the US government, and it, too, plays a major role in efforts to prevent disease and also drug abuse. The CDC works with health departments and community-based organizations, and it funds efforts to implement evidence-based prevention programs. One effort is the Prescription Drug Overdose: Prevention for States program, which provides state health departments with resources and support to develop preventive interventions to combat prescription drug overdoses. The CDC funds twenty-nine states through the program. By 2019 the agency had given these states amounts ranging from $750,000 to $1 million to develop prevention programs focused on key areas. One such area is improving prescription drug monitoring programs, which are electronic databases that track a state's prescriptions of controlled substances such as opioids. Another CDC effort is providing technical assistance (such as information, training, and funding) to communities with a high incidence of opioid abuse to better understand what works to prevent opioid overdoses.

The CDC has also created the Rx Awareness campaign to increase awareness about the risks involved with prescription opioids. The campaign creates evidence-based resources and materials such as infographics, videos, radio spots, online ads, social media, posters, and billboards. For example, the campaign's billboards, posters, and online ads feature a photo of a prescription medicine bottle accompanied by a warning that opioids can be addictive and dangerous.

The CDC's Rx Awareness website also provides real-life stories of people whose lives were devastated by the misuse of prescription opioids. One of these people is Cortney Lovell, a recovered heroin addict who now works to help others recover from addiction. "I am hoping to use the insights I've gained in the last 10 years of recovery to give others the same hope and encouragement I received," Lovell writes on the site. "I know how profound it can be to have people share their own experiences with you, knowing that they may have gone through even worse, yet are living full lives."[69]

Efforts by the National Institutes of Health

With the opioid epidemic in full swing, there is a pressing need for research studies that can help develop effective prevention efforts. One such study is being conducted by the National Institutes of Health (NIH). The HEALing Communities Study began in 2019 and aims to reduce opioid-related deaths by 40 percent over the course of three years. The study will examine prevention and treatment interventions, including distributing naloxone and providing addiction treatment to people who are incarcerated. The multiyear study has received more than $350 million and is being carried out by the NIH in partnership with SAMHSA, which provides support for many of the prevention, treatment, and recovery services that will be provided.

The ambitious HEALing Communities Study will be carried out via four research sites in states that have been hit especially hard by the opioid epidemic: the University of Kentucky in Lexington; Boston Medical Center in Massachusetts; Columbia University in New York City; and Ohio State University in Columbus. Each site will work with at least fifteen local communities to measure the effects of prevention, treatment, and recovery interventions. The study will track the efforts of each community to increase the use of MAT for opioid addiction, increase treatment retention (the time individuals stay in treatment) beyond six months, provide recovery support services, expand the distribution of naloxone, and reduce the incidence of opioid addiction and overdose deaths in the community. "The evidence generated through the HEALing Communities Study will help communities nationwide address the opioid crisis at the local level," says Volkow. "By testing and evaluating interventions where they are needed the most, we hope to show how researchers, providers, and communities can come together and finally bring an end to this devastating public health crisis."[70]

The study is part of the NIH Helping to End Addiction Long-Term (NIH HEAL) Initiative. The initiative involves a transagency effort to speed research and develop scientific solutions to the opioid crisis. Thus far, the NIH HEAL Initiative has awarded tens of millions of dollars in research grants and other funding. This helps hundreds of projects nationwide that are focused on a variety of approaches to prevent opioid addiction, including pain management and treatment for opioid addiction.

One program is specifically focused on preventing at-risk adolescents from becoming addicted to opioids. These include American Indians/Alaska Natives, homeless people, youths in the juvenile or criminal justice system, and families in the child welfare system. The program involves a series of studies to develop and test prevention strategies aimed at older adolescents and young adults in these at-risk groups. The NIH spells out the pressing need for such studies: "Older adolescents and young adults (ages 16–30) are at the highest risk for initiation of opioid use, opioid misuse, opioid use disorder (OUD), and death from overdose, and there are no evidence-based interventions to prevent opioid use disorder."[72] The prevention strategies and interventions developed by the program will be delivered in health care settings, including emergency rooms, school health centers, mental health facilities, and substance abuse behavioral health treatment facilities.

More Work to Be Done

Experts agree that more efforts toward prevention, including research on intervention efforts, are sorely needed. According to the CDC, it will take a concerted effort on the part of everyone involved. "Whether you are a healthcare provider, first responder, law enforcement officer, public health official, or community member, the opioid epidemic is likely affecting you and your community," says the CDC. "No matter who you are, you can take action to end the opioid overdose epidemic ravaging the United States."[72]

Introduction: An Illicit, Deadly Drug

1. Foundation for a Drug-Free World, "The Truth About Heroin," 2015. www.drugfreeworld.org.
2. Ben Cimon, "A Suburban Heroin Addict Describes His Brush with Death and His Hopes for a Better Life," *Washington Post*, February 10, 2014. www.washingtonpost.com.
3. Daniel Ciccarone, "Streets of Pain," Medium, June 13, 2018. https://medium.com.

Chapter One: A Nationwide Problem

4. Quoted in Kate Vidinsky, "Opioid Crisis: This Doctor's Street-Level Views Could Change the Course of the Epidemic," University of California, San Francisco, June 12, 2018. www.ucsf.edu.
5. Quoted in Michel Martin, "How Do Illegal Drugs Cross the U.S.-Mexico Border?," *All Things Considered*, NPR, April 6, 2019. www.npr.org.
6. Congressional Research Service, *Heroin Trafficking in the United States*. Washington, DC: Congressional Research Service, 2019. https://crsreports.congress.gov.
7. Quoted in US Customs and Border Protection, "Brownsville Port of Entry CBP Officers Seize $205K in Narcotics at Brownsville and Matamoros International Bridge," January 22, 2020. www.cbp.gov.
8. Foundation for a Drug-Free World, "The Truth About Heroin."
9. Centers for Disease Control and Prevention, "Heroin," December 19, 2018. www.cdc.gov.
10. National Institute on Drug Abuse, "What Is the Scope of Heroin Use in the United States?," 2018. www.drugabuse.gov.
11. National Institute on Drug Abuse, "Heroin Use Is Rare in Prescription Drug Users," January 2018. www.drugabuse.gov.
12. Jesse Chapman, "Jesse," I Am Not Anonymous, 2015. www.iamnotanonymous.org.
13. Nicholette, "Nicholette," I Am Not Anonymous, 2015. www.iamnotanonymous.org.

14. Quoted in University of Southern California, "Teens Abusing Painkillers Are More Likely to Later Use Heroin," ScienceDaily, July 8, 2019. www.sciencedaily.com.

Chapter Two: The Stranglehold of Addiction

15. Deon, "Heroin Addiction: 'I Needed the Drug Just to Get By,'" National Institute on Drug Abuse. https://easyread.drug abuse.gov.

16. Quoted in David Allegretti, "Former Users Describe the First Time They Tried Heroin," *Vice*, November 6, 2015. www.vice .com.

17. Quoted in Shreeya Sinha, "Heroin Addiction Explained: How Opioids Hijack the Brain," *New York Times*, December 18, 2018. www.nytimes.com.

18. Quoted in Foundation for a Drug-Free World, "The Truth About Heroin."

19. American Addiction Centers, "The Mental Effects of Heroin: Short-Term and Long-Term," June 17, 2019. https://american addictioncenters.org.

20. Quoted in Chris Elkins, "What Does Heroin Feel Like?," Drug Rehab.com, May 18, 2018. www.drugrehab.com.

21. Sinha, "Heroin Addiction Explained."

22. American Addiction Centers, "The Mental Effects of Heroin."

23. Quoted in University at Buffalo, "How Relapse Happens: Opiates Reduce the Brain's Ability to Form, Maintain Synapses: Preclinical Research Was Focused on Revealing the Molecular Mechanisms Behind Addiction and Relapse," ScienceDaily, September 12, 2019. www.sciencedaily.com.

24. Quoted in University at Buffalo, "How Relapse Happens."

25. Quoted in Elkins, "What Does Heroin Feel Like?"

26. Quoted in Elkins, "What Does Heroin Feel Like?"

27. Deon, "Heroin Addiction."

28. Quoted in Sarah T. Williams, "What's It Really Like to Withdraw from Heroin and Painkillers?," *Minnesota Post*, February 14, 2014. www.minnpost.com.

29. American Addiction Centers, "The Mental Effects of Heroin."

30. Quoted in Nicholas Kristof, "These Newborn Babies Cry for Drugs, Not Milk," *New York Times*, September 7, 2019. www .nytimes.com.

Chapter Three: Heroin's Destructive Health Effects

31. Quoted in Jessica Ravitz and Gena Somra, "'This Is Skid Row': What Two Current Heroin Addicts Want You to Know," CNN, October 27, 2017. www.cnn.com.

32. Quoted in Allegretti, "Former Users Describe the First Time They Tried Heroin."

33. Quoted in Cari Nierenberg, "10 Interesting Facts About Heroin," Live Science, October 27, 2016. www.livescience.com.

34. National Institute on Drug Abuse, "Research Reports: Heroin," June 2018. www.drugabuse.gov.

35. Quoted in Nicole Napoli, "Opioid Use Associated with Dramatic Rise in Dangerous Heart Infection," American College of Cardiology, March 6, 2019. www.acc.org.

36. Ken Seeley, "The Dangers of Skin Abscess from Injecting Heroin," Ken Seeley Communities, September 13, 2019. https:// kenseeleycommunities.com.

37. Rebecca Nightingale, "Screening Heroin Smokers Attending Community Drug Clinics for Change in Lung Function: A Cohort Study," Science Direct, November 2019. www.science direct.com.

38. Foundation for a Drug-Free World, "The Truth About Heroin."

39. Quoted in Jason Silverstein, "When an Overdose Doesn't Kill You," *Vice*, July 3, 2017. www.vice.com.

40. Quoted in Silverstein, "When an Overdose Doesn't Kill You."

41. Quoted in Maia Szalavitz, "The Mysterious Consequences of Repeatedly Overdosing on Opioids," *Vice,* June 5, 2019. www.vice.com.

42. Steven Dowshen, "Heroin," TeensHealth, 2018. https://kid shealth.org.

43. Foundations Recovery Network, "Dangers of Drug Overdose," 2020. https://dualdiagnosis.org.

44. Quoted in Claire Galofaro, "After the Overdose: A Family's Journey into Grief and Guilt," *AP News*, January 28, 2019. https://apnews.com.

45. Quoted in Ravitz and Somra, "'This Is Skid Row.'"

Chapter Four: The Challenges of Treatment and Recovery

46. Quoted in Williams, "What's It Really Like to Withdraw from Heroin and Painkillers?"

47. Abbey Zorzi, "Abbey Zorzi, 22," *Just Think Twice*. www.just thinktwice.gov.

48. Zorzi, "Abbey Zorzi, 22."

49. Zorzi, "Abbey Zorzi, 22."

50. Zorzi, "Abbey Zorzi, 22."

51. Zorzi, "Abbey Zorzi, 22."

52. Quoted in Serena Gordon, "U.S. Heroin Use Nearly Doubled over Two Decades," *WebMD*, February 11, 2020. www.web md.com.

53. Quoted in Brianna Ehley and Rachel Roubein, "'I'm Trying Not to Die Right Now': Why Opioid-Addicted Patients Are Still Searching for Help," *Politico*, January 22, 2019. www.politico .com.

54. Quoted in Sinha, "Heroin Addiction Explained."

55. Quoted in Sinha, "Heroin Addiction Explained."

56. Quoted in US Department of Health and Human Services, Office of the Surgeon General, *Facing Addiction in America: The Surgeon General's Spotlight on Opioids*. Washington, DC: US Department of Health and Human Services, 2018. https://addiction.surgeongeneral.gov.

57. Quoted in German Lopez, "A Lost Decade and $200,000: One Dad's Crusade to Save His Daughters from Addiction," *Vox*, October 9, 2019. www.vox.com.

58. Francie Diep, "There's a Gold-Standard Treatment for Opioid Addiction, One of America's Top Killers: What Keeps Treatment Centers from Using It?," *Pacific Standard,* April 22, 2019. https://psmag.com.

59. Quoted in Lopez, "A Lost Decade and $200,000."

60. Quoted in Ehley and Roubein, "'I'm Trying Not to Die Right Now.'"

Chapter Five: Stopping Heroin Addiction Before It Starts

61. Nora Volkow, "The Importance of Prevention in Addressing the Opioid Crisis," *Nora's Blog*, National Institute on Drug Abuse, June 27, 2019. www.drugabuse.gov.

62. Quoted in Laura Ungar, "School Districts Double Down on Drug Testing, Targeting Even Middle Schoolers," *U.S. News & World Report*, September 5, 2019. www.usnews.com.

63. Quoted in Patrick Nothaft, "Athletes, Parents, Coaches React to Michigan School's New Random Drug Testing," M-Live, January 20, 2020. www.mlive.com.

64. American Civil Liberties Union, "Just Say No to Random Drug Testing: A Guide for Students," 2020. www.aclu.org.

65. Quoted in Mary Fetzer, "Drug Testing in Schools: What You and Your Student Need to Know," *ParentMap* (blog), October 19, 2016. https://www.parentmap.com.

66. Quoted in Sarah Vander Schaaff, "Opioid Deaths Prompt Ohio to Reimagine Classroom Lessons, Starting with Kindergarten," *Washington Post*, April 22, 2018. www.washington post.com.

67. Quoted in Vander Schaaff, "Opioid Deaths Prompt Ohio to Reimagine Classroom Lessons, Starting with Kindergarten."

68. Campus Drug Prevention, "How to Help a Friend." www .campusdrugprevention.gov.

69. Quoted in Centers for Disease Control and Prevention, "Rx Awareness: Cortney," September 22, 2017. www.cdc.gov.

70. Quoted in National Institutes of Health, "NIH Funds Study in Four States to Reduce Opioid Related Deaths by 40 Percent over Three Years," April 18, 2019. www.nih.gov.

71. National Institutes of Health, "Preventing At-Risk Adolescents Transitioning into Adulthood from Developing Opioid Use Disorder," November 26, 2019. https://heal.nih.gov.

72. Centers for Disease Control and Prevention, "Rx Awareness: About the Campaign," March 12, 2019. www.cdc.gov.

American Society of Addiction Medicine (ASAM)
www.asam.org

ASAM seeks to improve the quality of addiction treatment, increase access to it, and support research and prevention efforts. Its website offers articles, fact sheets, and other publications about heroin use, the abuse of other opioids, and addiction.

Centers for Disease Control and Prevention (CDC)
www.cdc.gov

The CDC, which is America's leading health protection agency, seeks to control disease, injury, and disability. Numerous articles, fact sheets, and policy statements about heroin and other opioids can be found on its website.

Drug Enforcement Administration (DEA)—www.dea.gov

The DEA is the top federal drug law enforcement agency in the United States. Its website links to a separate site called Just Think Twice (www.justthinktwice.gov) that is designed for teenagers. A good collection of information about heroin and other opioids can be found on the site, including real-life student addiction stories, fact sheets, news articles, and more.

Foundation for a Drug-Free World—www.drugfreeworld.org

The Foundation for a Drug-Free World seeks to empower young people with factual information about drugs so they can make smart decisions and live drug free. Its website offers a wealth of information about the dangers and risks associated with drug abuse, including a booklet on heroin and personal testimonial videos.

I Am Not Anonymous—www.iamnotanonymous.org

I Am Not Anonymous seeks to end the stigma associated with addiction, spread awareness of addiction as a disease (rather than as a moral failing), and help the millions who remain untreated by sharing stories of hope. The website features a number of power-ful stories of addicts who have turned their lives around.

National Institute on Drug Abuse (NIDA)
www.drugabuse.gov

NIDA seeks to advance research on the causes and effects of drug use and addiction and to apply that knowledge to improve people's health. Its website links to a separate NIDA for Teens site (https://teens.drugabuse.gov/teens) that is especially de-signed for young people and provides great information about drug abuse and addiction, including heroin.

Partnership for Drug-Free Kids—https://drugfree.org

The Partnership for Drug-Free Kids is dedicated to supporting families who are addressing substance abuse and addiction. Its website's search engine produces numerous publications about heroin and other types of opioids.

Substance Abuse and Mental Health Services Administration (SAMHSA)—www.samhsa.gov

SAMHSA seeks to reduce the impact of substance abuse on America's communities. The website's search engine produces numerous articles and fact sheets as well as a downloadable bro-chure called "Tips for Teens: The Truth About Heroin."

Books

John Allen, *The Opioid Crisis*. San Diego: ReferencePoint, 2020.

John Cashin, *The Heroin Crisis*. Broomall, PA: Mason Crest, 2018.

Sabine Cherenfant, ed., *The Opioid Crisis.* New York: Greenhaven, 2019.

Beth Macy, *Dopesick: Dealers, Doctors, and the Drug Company That Addicted America*. New York: Back Bay, 2019.

Sam Quinones, *Dreamland.* Nashville: Parnassus, 2019.

Eva Summerhill, *Confessions of a Heroin Addict's Mother: A Memoir of Self-Reflection*. Seattle: Amazon Digital Services, 2020, Kindle.

Christine Wilcox, *Opioid Abuse*. San Diego: ReferencePoint, 2019.

Internet Sources

Anya Edney and Lauren Etter, "The Opioid Crisis," Bloomberg, August 26, 2019. www.bloomberg.com.

Gaby Galvin, "The Deadliest Drugs in America in 2017," *U.S. News & World Report*, October 29, 2019. www.usnews.com.

Georgea Kovanis, "She Was Prostituting, Pregnant, Doing Drugs by 14. Now, Taylor Girl Fights to Save Her Own Life," *Detroit Free Press*, November 3, 2019. www.freep.com.

National Institute on Drug Abuse, "Heroin," NIDA for Teens, 2019. https://teens.drugabuse.gov.

Rachel Rippetoe and Niamh McDonnell, "Hub of Heroin: Portraits of a Teen, an Addict and a 'Mayor' amid South Bronx Heroin Epidemic," Juvenile Justice Information Exchange, December 20, 2019. https://jjie.org.

Shreeya Sinha, "Heroin Addiction Explained: How Opioids Hijack the Brain," *New York Times*, December 18, 2018. www.nytimes .com.

University of Southern California, "Teens Abusing Painkillers Are More Likely to Later Use Heroin," Science Daily, July 8, 2019. www.sciencedaily.com.

US Department of Health and Human Services, "Opioids and Adolescents," May 13, 2019. www.hhs.gov.

Aubrey Whelan and Jeremy Roebuck, "Two Friends Shared Heroin in a KFC Bathroom. One Died, One Went to Prison. Their Families Are Picking Up the Pieces," *Philadelphia Inquirer*, June 6, 2019. www.inquirer.com.

PICTURE CREDITS

Peggy J. Parks has written nearly 160 educational books for young people. She holds a bachelor of science degree from Aquinas College in Grand Rapids, Michigan, where she graduated *magna cum laude*. Parks lives in the lakeshore town of Muskegon, Michigan.